AN INSPECTOR DEVLIN MYSTERY

J. S. COOK

A COLD-BLOODED SCOUNDREL

A Brandon Original Paperback

First published in Britain and Ireland in 2005 by
Brandon
an imprint of Mount Eagle Publications, Dingle, Co. Kerry, Ireland
and
Unit 3 Olympia Trading Estate, Coburg Road, London N22 6TZ, England

2 4 6 8 10 9 7 5 3 1

Mount Eagle Publications receives support from
the Arts Council/An Chomhairle Ealaíon.

ISBN 0 86322 336 2

Cover design: id Communications, Tralee
Typesetting by Red Barn Publishing, Skeagh, Skibbereen
Printed in the UK

For Paul:
my companion, my inspiration and my lucky star

CHAPTER ONE

THE DEAD MAN was smiling. He was lying in a narrow defile, a lane joining two filthy East End streets. He had been dead a while, judging by the condition of the body and the colour of his skin: a dusky greyish-green, shading to black where the blood had pooled and settled in his tissues. The eyes were wide open and bulging with the burden of post-mortem gases; the hands were held with the palms facing down at his sides, the fingers clenched. His throat had been cut.

There was something underneath his fingernails, something dark and viscous and oily-looking; all his hair was gone. Devlin bent low to sniff the dead man's open mouth, steeling himself against the stink of charred flesh.

"What are you doing that for?" Constable Freddie Collins, lately of the London Metropolitan Police and of Pimlico, respectively, hovered over the corpse, keeping well out of the way of Inspector Phillip Devlin, also of the London Metropolitan Police, but rumoured to be living in Brixton.

"Checking for poison. Depending on which one, sometimes you can smell it." Devlin, absorbed in scraping under the deceased's fingernails, didn't look up.

"It's a bit weird, Inspector." Freddie tilted his head to one side. "How come he's smiling?"

"Heat, from the fire." Devlin deftly extracted a sample from under the fingernails, swiped it on to a small piece of paper. "The heat dries the muscles out and makes them contract. Then again, he might have been poisoned. You never can tell. Bag?"

Freddie snapped open a brown paper bag and put it into Devlin's outstretched hand. "Bag." He paused. "But it's really odd."

Devlin tucked the paper into the bag and folded the bag carefully. "What's odd, Constable? The fact that someone's tried to burn him to a crisp or the fact that they also shoved something up his nostrils?" He pushed Freddie aside none too gently and bent down. There were some in the Yard who laughed at Devlin for his hobbies, but his habit of collecting all the rag-tag bits and bobs from a crime scene had helped out in the past. "You never know where a man's nostrils will lead you," Devlin said comfortably.

"Cripes!" Freddie was hovering again. "That's. . ."

"Paper and black powder," Devlin said. "Fireworks."

"Up his nose?"

"Up his nose?" Devlin waited. "Never seen that before."

Freddie shook his head. "Rough way to blow a man's nose."

"Constable," Devlin said.

"Sorry, Sir."

Devlin pulled back the unbuttoned shirt. "Take a look." In the middle of the dead man's chest there was a thumbprint. In blood.

"Must have been done after he was already dead," Freddie said. "Has to be. Who'd stand still and let someone do that to them? Unless he did it himself."

"He wasn't killed here, that's for sure. There's no blood on the wall. So his throat was cut elsewhere, and the killer brought the body here." Devlin dragged his eyes away from the thumbprint. "He's come back again."

Freddie understood. "But he's. . ."

"We never made it stick. He was free to go." Devlin got up, wincing as his knee joints popped.

"He wouldn't dare."

Devlin shook his head. "Wouldn't he? The last I heard he'd emigrated to Australia. Going to make his fortune in the gold mines." He tapped Freddie's arm. "Go round to the pub and fetch the constables back." Devlin had sent them away on the pretext of fetching him a jar of gin. He didn't actually drink gin, but he'd rather that than three or four large-footed Peelers stomping all over his crime. "It's better if Mr Whoever isn't exposed to the scrutiny of the popular press."

He waited till Freddie had gone, then bent low over the body and stared hard at the thumbprint.

It never got any easier.

* * *

It never got any easier.

Devlin tried to remember (not for the first time) why he was here. Of course it was tradition, and a custom of his, almost a punishment of sorts, that he turn up here every year on this date and reflect upon her grave, to remember. Ten years ago the prostitute Elizabeth Hobbs had died a violent and gruesome death, courtesy of John Whittaker. Ten years, and every year Devlin made himself come here and remember her. If only he'd been quicker, if only he'd done more to save her, if only he'd been able to find Whittaker before Whittaker found her. He put on his hat, knelt down and pressed his lips to the cold stone: a charity job, just her name chiselled into a block of ordinary granite. They'd passed the hat round, Devlin and the others, compelled by an obscure sense of mercy and slightly ashamed of themselves. "I'm sorry." He could hardly force the words past the lump in his throat, and even though he was alone in the cemetery, he was grateful for the driving October rain that effectively hid his tears. How unseemly that a hardened copper should be crying like a little girl. If the others at the Yard saw it they wouldn't believe it. As far as they knew, Devlin had no such command of human emotion; he was an instrument that played only one note.

He hailed a horse-drawn cab just outside the cemetery

gates and climbed inside, his mind curiously empty of sensation. His gloved hands lay in his lap, and his dark eyes gazed at nothing. For the duration of the ride back to Scotland Yard, he deliberately concentrated on the sense of emptiness – he knew if he didn't, he would weep again, and that would never do.

* * *

"Sir?" Constable Collins stood a respectful distance from Devlin's desk. Although he was not noted for his mental acuity, even Collins knew that Devlin was not himself today, and he hesitated to push where he knew he was not wanted. He cleared he throat and began again: "Sir?"

"Yes?" Devlin had been staring at the pile of paper on his desk for half an hour, willing his mind into activity, but so far he'd had no luck. He'd have to stop going to the cemetery, he thought – it wasn't doing him any good, and it certainly wasn't doing Elizabeth Hobbs any good, seeing how she'd been in the ground this ten years and her murderer gone free on a technicality because of his position in society and his family's money. Devlin ought to concentrate his energies on this new case, instead of turning over old stones.

"I thought you'd like some tea, Sir. Bloody wet and cold out there today." Collins laid down a thick mug of the steaming brew and stood back again. The inspector, who hadn't moved so much as an inch, was still occupied with his internal considerations, whatever they were. Collins hoped to be an inspector himself someday, and he wondered precisely what sorts of things men like Devlin were wont to think about. Collins, a mere twenty-two to Devlin's thirty-five, had no real idea.

Devlin blinked, seeming to draw himself back from a great distance, and stared at Collins as if he'd just then materialised from out of the floor. "What?" He scratched his head in a distracted manner, further disturbing his hair which, when wet, tended to arrange itself into astonishing cowlicks and curlicues which were not at all conducive to the habitual dignity of a Yard inspector. Collins allowed himself the hint of a smile. He liked it when Devlin allowed himself to become just that little bit disarranged, because, truth be told, Collins fancied his superior and thought that Devlin was a real cracker. But he'd never repeat this to Devlin.

Since 1885, no man in London of Freddie's proclivities could rest easy in his off-hours. For the past four years, the frivolity of Freddie and his fellows had been dying a painful and protracted death. *Piss on Labouchere and his bloody old Amendment to the Act, anyway. It was getting so a man couldn't have a bit of harmless fun.* There was no getting round it, and who wanted to end up in Reading Gaol or Pentonville? Freddie hadn't the leg strength for the treadmill. He sighed gently.

"Something wrong, Constable?" Devlin picked up the tea and examined it intently before bringing the mug to his mouth and sipping it with great enjoyment. Collins was a fool, but a fool who understood the art of the teapot.

"No, Sir." Collins withdrew a piece of paper from underneath his left elbow and passed it across the desk to Devlin. "Thought you might want to see this, Sir."

Devlin took the paper and examined it carefully. "I am down on whores," he read aloud, "and I shan't quit ripping them –" He tossed the paper on to the growing pile at the front of his desk and treated Collins to a look of utter contempt. "For the love of God!" he said. "Where did you dig this up, eh? Been foraging in the rubbish bins again?"

Merely a year or two ago, yet Devlin remembered it as if it were yesterday. They all did. Bad enough that Jack the Ripper had left Mary Kelly in pieces, but they – Devlin, the Yard, everybody – had let him get away. He sat back and pressed his fingers against his eyes, still sore and gritty from a sleepless night. If he had a shilling for every East End delinquent who fancied himself a master criminal, he could safely hand in his warrant card without fear of destitution or the workhouse.

"It's not left over from the Ripper, Sir." Collins shifted his not inconsiderable weight to his other foot and regarded Devlin with what he probably thought was a weather eye. "Just came in this morning. Young lad brought it round, he did. Said to give it to Inspector Devlin."

Devlin was too old and too experienced to allow himself the luxury of a wide-eyed expression of shock – but something deep inside him recoiled whenever he remembered the Ripper. He fumbled in his desk for his cigarettes, struck a match with rather more of a flourish than was strictly necessary and hoped Collins didn't notice the overt shaking of his hands.

But Collins had. "You all right, Sir?"

Devlin treated him to a withering look. "Of course, I'm

all right!" He drew hard on his cigarette. "Didn't sleep well last night," he muttered.

"Sorry to hear that, Sir." Collins refused to meet Devlin's eyes and fixed his gaze stolidly on the worn carpet between his feet.

"Mind your own bloody business!" Devlin snapped, and instantly regretted it. "Look, Collins . . ." He sighed noisily and allowed his gaze to rest upon the tall young constable. Freddie Collins looked like something off a Peak Freans tin, if you caught him in the right light, or else an hyperbolic illustration of "The Glories of the Empire". He was a shade over six feet tall, with long bones that in another man might have been lanky and ungainly. His hair was a particularly curly blond, lighter at the ends, as if he'd just now got back from a sojourn in the South Seas. His eyes were brown, but not the deep, nearly black of Devlin's own. Freddie's eyes were the colour of warm hazelnut cream, and his careful mouth always managed to retain the hint of a smirk. In another set of circumstances, Freddie might have felt at home in the crimson uniform of a cavalry officer. He had that sort of bearing. Devlin had no idea how Freddie had managed to become a Peeler.

"I'm not sure what we've got, exactly," Devlin managed to say. He took another sip of his tea. By God, how did Collins always manage to get it just so? Piping hot with just a hint of sugar and generous amounts of milk. He wondered when the throbbing in his skull was going to subside. "You've got to keep an eye out for these kinds of copycats. Every man-jack on the docks fancies himself some sort of dark character, if only for the pleasure of his own vanity." It was one of the longest speeches Devlin had ever made, and it exhausted him.

"Something else, too." Freddie gave him another piece of paper. "That odd fellow who works in the laboratory sent this up."

"It's about the corpse we found." Devlin scanned the note quickly. "Damn," he murmured. "You'll never guess what was under his fingernails." Devlin peered at the note. "Hair ointment made with ambergris. Hmph."

"Made out of whales, isn't it?" Freddie asked.

"It's bloody expensive, is what it is. Not too many in Whitechapel or Seven Dials who'd toss a bob for this." Devlin thought of something. "Not everybody can smell it, either."

Freddie looked suitably blank. "Then how did that laboratory fellow know it was there?"

"I expect he can smell it." Devlin wasn't entirely sure how the morgue attendant knew to isolate such compounds.

Freddie thought for a moment. "Oh, right. Can you?"

"Yes, I can. They use it in toiletries, mostly. It's the secretion of a sperm whale." Devlin hastened to explain: "I read a lot."

"Beggin' your pardon, Inspector," interrupted Barnicott, a very junior constable from downstairs with startling orange hair and a veritable blizzard of freckles. "The Chief says he's wantin' to see yer in his office, like."

"Did he say what it was about?"

"No idea, Sir. Said for me to fetch you." The lad sketched a quick glance at Collins and scuttled away down the corridor like a startled land crab.

"Think it's about the note?" Collins shot a look at Devlin. "Or perhaps Old Brassie's got his knickers in a twist again."

"Constable." Devlin sounded a warning note: he, like all the others, knew Sir Neville Alcock's nickname among the force, but that didn't mean he had to countenance its use among the junior officers. "Don't let me hear you say it again." The term "Brassie" had been coined by some semi-literate wag who thought that a man with a surname like "All Cock" must have a nether member made of brass. Of course, the name had stuck, to the merriment of all concerned, and even those youngest of the constables who were just entering the service were necessarily briefed on its proper uses and abuses.

Devlin paused to straighten his necktie and attempted to smooth down his hair with the aid of his palms, but to no effect. He glanced at himself in the small shaving mirror mounted over his filing cabinet: tired eyes, face too pale from lack of sleep, shoulders already sagging even though it was barely eleven in the morning.

"You look fine, Sir." Collins appeared behind him, smiling gently. "Perfectly all right." Privately, he remarked to himself that Devlin needed a good sleep, a hot bath and a hot meal and then a bloody good screw, not necessarily in that order.

Devlin's eyes met those of the constable in the mirror, and for a moment something indefinable passed between them, something wistful and sweet. "I should only be about half an hour, depending." Devlin tossed this off over his shoulder as he flew out the door. "Make another pot of tea?"

Freddie Collins grinned and set about doing just that.

* * *

Sir Neville Alcock was fat: not plump or merry or even well fleshed, but huge, enormous, a vast rolling bulk of a man with a belly the approximate size of some larger species of barrel. His hands were little, fat and doughy as suet, and his head sat atop the great mound of his body like a jack-o'-lantern. All in all, he seemed to be composed of several intersecting spheres, rather like a snowman.

"Devlin."

Devlin sagged visibly. Sir Neville could manage to fit more disappointment into the two syllables of the inspector's name than most people; surely this couldn't be good news. "Sir?" He took the glass of brandy that Sir Neville offered, taking care not to quaff it too hastily, and sat down at Sir Neville's indication that he should do so.

"I'm beginning to think Jack the Ripper has come back." Alcock looked him up and down. "We've had strange happenings of late, Devlin."

"Like what, Sir?" Devlin gazed into the brandy, warming the glass between his palms.

"There's been talk," Alcock said. "I dispatched someone to see about it. Just off Mitre Square in the East End." He pushed a map across the table; a small square area was carefully marked off in red pencil. "The body you attended wasn't the only one." He indicated the map. "An hour ago a second body was found. I sent Inspector Abernathy, but he thinks it's a copycat, someone trying to be Jack the Ripper."

The corners of Devlin's mouth curled. "Abernathy knows this how, exactly? He wasn't at the first scene. I've not even filed my report yet. With all due respect, Sir, even you don't know all the details. What's Abernathy's like?"

Alcock grunted. "Eviscerated, face carved up and what appears to be a cigar burn on the forehead." He flipped open a file folder. "He's very punctual about reporting all the facts. Wants to make sure we have all the information at hand." Alcock shot a pointed look at Devlin. "An hour. And he's got the body in the morgue already."

Which meant that Abernathy hadn't even examined the scene properly. Abernathy had probably done a quick walk-through, drawn his own conclusions and sent the body on its way. "The body's here?"

"Abernathy made sure of it."

"Abernathy is a lazy man and a bloody idiot."

"It's not strictly your case, Devlin, so don't get shirty with me. I've not even assigned you. I might assign Abernathy."

"Abernathy." He was beginning to sound like an idiot, even to himself.

"Well, you'd best do something about it, then. I'm not interested in another panic like we had with the Ripper. I want this killer in custody. I'm not terribly fussy about which one of you manages to do it." Alcock stood up and waddled over to the window.

"He likes to burn things," Devlin said carefully. "Not buildings, not property. People. Hair, fingernails, skin. He likes the smell of burning protein." Devlin had seen him do a rabbit once, while it was still alive.

"Who likes it?"

Devlin's necktie was strangling him; he made his voice deliberately light. "John Whittaker."

"Whittaker?" Alcock laughed nastily. "No, I don't believe this is Whittaker, Inspector. He wouldn't dare! And anyway, he's in Australia."

"No." Devlin felt sickness rising in his gorge like bile. "He's not." He didn't wait for Alcock's question. "A bloody thumbprint, Sir, on the victim's sternum. Placed there after he was dead. When I went back to the scene, Elizabeth Hobbs was gutted like a market calf, her hair had been burned away, and there was a bloody thumbprint on her thigh."

"Rubbish," Alcock growled. It sounded like a slow mountain moving its bowels.

"I know him." Devlin was on his feet. "It's the way Elizabeth Hobbs was done. No, he didn't cut this one up, but in every other aspect it's the same."

Alcock flicked a fat hand towards the door. "If that's all you've got, then go."

Devlin opened his mouth to argue but thought better of it. Sir Neville was hardly even-tempered at the best of times.

He remembered Elizabeth Hobbs: fourteen years old and already habituated to the streets. A whore, a common doxy, procured long ago by someone who'd wanted a taste of virgin flesh and was willing to pay for it. She wasn't the first of her kind, and Devlin knew she wouldn't be the last, but Whittaker had a specific grudge against her. The official story was that she'd infected Whittaker with syphilis. If it were true, it would be reason enough to want revenge. Devlin wasn't sure how long it took syphilitics to die. Perhaps Elizabeth was already so far gone that her murderer had been doing her a favour . . . no, that was too easy. She must have come into contact with Whittaker in the first two years after her own infection or it never would have spread to him. Or perhaps Devlin had miscalculated, and she was further gone than that. She'd worn a wig the day Devlin had met her, a cheap wig made of dyed horsehair that sat awkwardly on her head like a small dead animal.

"It makes your hair fall out," he said.

"What does?" Alcock sloshed more brandy into his own glass.

"Syphilis."

"I'm not a doctor," Alcock said, "and neither are you." He inhaled deeply. "This needs to be kept quiet or there's going to be panic in the streets. That's all we bloody well need, another panic."

"Quite so, Sir." Devlin cleared his throat. "So I'll bring some of the constables into it, as well?"

Sir Neville turned and glared at him. "God damn it, man! Weren't you listening?" His fat hands worked awkwardly at the air directly in front of his chest. "I want to keep it quiet. Find out who this blackguard is and if he's genuine, or if some copycat thinks to have himself some fun. Use that young Collins. He's thick enough, but I daresay his lack of brains will keep his mouth shut."

Devlin sagged with relief. "Right," he said, with as much crispness as he could muster. "I'll get on it immediately, Sir."

He laid down the brandy glass and stood, eager to make his exit. He was within blessed sight of the doorway.

"Oh, Devlin?"

Devlin composed his face into appropriate lines before turning round. "Sir?"

"Er . . . my wife is having a little tea dance on Saturday."

Devlin stifled a groan by driving his teeth forcibly into his bottom lip.

"She wanted me to invite you."

Devlin had a momentary vision: being wheeled gracefully around the room in Sir Neville's grip, to the strains of a violin, a cello or two, tea and finger sandwiches afterwards in the sitting room.

"My daughter Phoebe will be there. She's been at her auntie's in Swansea these three months, and I know she will want to make your acquaintance." Sir Neville paused, wrinkling his walrus-like moustache. "Not, er . . . married, are you, Devlin?"

"No, Sir, not yet." Devlin coughed – he was about as near to marriage as Gibraltar was to the South Pole. "But it's definitely in my future plans, Sir."

Damn!

"Ah . . . well, you will want to meet my Phoebe, then."

Devlin imagined what this paragon must look like: four feet tall and five feet wide, with great rolls of fat barely concealed beneath some hideous haute couture creation. Perhaps there was a way to escape what seemed to be his preordained fate. He might arrange to have Freddie Collins push him over the Tower Bridge. The foetid water of the Thames would kill him instantly.

"Thank you, Sir." Devlin took his leave as gracefully as quickness would allow.

CHAPTER TWO

THE SUDDEN FLARE of a lit match illuminated the small rooms; Devlin drew hard on his cigarette and went to push open one of his windows. He hadn't slept properly for ten bloody years now. At times like these, he was glad he lived alone, for there was no one to see or comment on his bizarre hours or the fact that he sometimes started up out of a sound sleep, a scream of horror dying in his throat. He was vaguely ashamed of his reactions. He knew better: getting personally involved in cases was the sort of mistake a green constable might make, not a seasoned inspector. He should be better than this, and he would be if the criminal weren't Whittaker.

He knew Whittaker, knew how smart Whittaker was, or

at least how clever he had been before syphilis had begun to rot his brains. He'd been in Australia, sure enough, but the climate didn't agree with him. It was too hot and too dry and there were biting things and stinging things, and all the plants and animals were poisonous and ugly. His mother had probably begged him to go, get out from underfoot or at least away from scandal. It's what Whittaker Senior would have wanted, but he had conveniently died of an apoplectic fit some months before Whittaker's case ever came to trial. Too much for him, the doctors had said. His heart couldn't take it. The truly sad thing – for John Whittaker – was that his father had died without ever seeking reconciliation and without ever changing the terms of his will. Since Devlin had been the arresting officer, it was Devlin's fault that Whittaker's father was dead, in which case Whittaker was probably looking for Devlin and wanting very much to burn Devlin's hair and put a bloody thumbprint somewhere on Devlin's person. The body they'd found in the alley was likely just a way for Whittaker to discharge some measure of his rage.

Devlin rubbed his hand over his tired face, his fingers scraping on stubble, and leaned against the windowsill. The night air was cold, but it was a good cold, and it helped to blow the nasty dreams out of his head, the ones that came just as he was falling asleep, when his ability to tell fact from illusory deception was deadened by exhaustion. He wondered what Freddie Collins was doing this time of night. The mantel clock said it was just gone half past eleven. Did Freddie have friends that he went out with, drinking in the pubs or chasing pretty little doxies in Piccadilly Circus? It was hard to imagine him sitting at home alone. Were his parents still alive? Had he any siblings? What did a lad like Freddie do on cool October nights when his daylight duties were all effectively discharged? He'd been assigned to Devlin for a year, ever since he joined the force, so perhaps Devlin should know him better than he did.

Right at that moment, Freddie Collins was in a pub, but not the sort of pub that Devlin might have imagined, and it wasn't doxies he was chasing. Well, Freddie admitted, he wasn't chasing anyone tonight, which wasn't like him – he wondered if he had lost his touch. No, he thought, as he brought his cigarette to his lips, it wasn't that. His mind was entirely on Inspector Devlin.

The inspector hadn't been himself today, and Freddie wondered whether Devlin was sick or merely tired and overworked. The warm brown eyes creased with tender mirth as Freddie imagined myriad ways of making his dear inspector feel much better – things Devlin had probably never thought of, much less heard of.

"Freddie, you raddled old whore, all alone tonight?" Dennis Dalziel tapped him on the shoulder as he went past in company with an elegant man who bore a certain resemblance to the solicitor Reginald Harker. The older man turned and gave Freddie a wink and a smile before disappearing into the evening with Dennis.

Thank God for the Peacock, Freddie thought. He practically had the bleeding Amendment to the Act memorised, or at least, the parts that applied to him: "Any male person who, in public or in private, commits any act of gross indecency with another male person shall be guilty of a misdemeanor, and being convicted thereof, shall be liable to be imprisoned for any term not exceeding one year with or without hard labour." It could effectively end his career with the Force, not to mention the twin spectres of imprisonment and hard labour. He shuddered, stubbing out his cigarette with an expression of distaste. Even the Peacock Club could, on times, be a most unsavoury venue for a young man who simply wanted the company of his own kind.

He fished out his watch: a quarter to midnight. Was Devlin asleep? And if so, would it be utterly criminal to wake him? Freddie sighed. What in God's name would he say once he'd got to Devlin's house? "I was sitting in this club I go to, called the Peacock? I kept thinking about you and I wondered if you'd mind a little bit of a kiss and a cuddle." Bloody scratch that one – he'd no desire to do hard time.

In his rooms elsewhere in London, Devlin fell into a fitful sleep and dreamed of Old Brassie's hefty daughter who had breasts like Easter hams. Towards the middle of the dream Freddie Collins rescued him, dressed in the scarlet uniform of a cavalry officer, Freddie put Devlin up on his horse and they clattered out of sight, a fairy-tale cliché.

Devlin turned over in his sleep and smiled.

Somewhere beyond his rooms, the Bow Bells chimed the hours, and the traffic of the London underworld moved slowly through its accustomed paces. Nothing touched him in his cocoon of sleep, as he rode with the dream of Freddie Collins on his ridiculous white charger.

* * *

"Sir."

Devlin blinked, desperate to clear his vision. He saw that he'd thrown the blankets off himself, and he wondered just how much writhing he'd had to be doing . . . and where the hell had Freddie Collins come from? "Collins. Where did you . . . what time is it?"

"Sir. Old Brassie sent me over here to rouse you. There's been another one. It's bad this time." In the pale morning light, Freddie's features were shadowed, haunted by a grievous shock. Judging by the expression on Freddie's face, it had to be very, very bad indeed.

Devlin set his bare feet upon the floor, dropped his head into his hands and rubbed his eyes with his palms. "How did you get in?"

"Your landlady let me in. She said you'd been up and pacing the floor till two this morning, so you were probably still sleeping." Freddie moved about Devlin's sparse lodgings, peering into the wardrobe and the dresser drawers, collecting articles of clothing with an appearance of great industry. He withdrew Devlin's shoes from underneath the bed and laid them out, selected a necktie from inside the wardrobe.

Devlin watched this performance with a feeling of immense irritation. "Constable, since when have you become my personal valet?" He was still tired, and his nightshirt hid the vestiges of a stubborn erection, courtesy of that damned dream. How in God's name could he stand up and let a younger constable see the precise tilt of his yardarm?

"Sorry, Sir, only Old Brassie said it was urgent."

"Well, go out on the landing while I get dressed, for God's sake." His dressing gown was within reach on the end of the bed, and Devlin caught it to him, belted it securely round his lean middle. "If you want to make yourself useful, go ask Mrs Taylor for some breakfast. I take it you've already eaten?"

Freddie sniffed, clearly wounded. "I wouldn't mind a muffin and a cup of tea," he said. "I've been up since half past five, and you know how Dobbin makes the tea."

Devlin didn't wait for him to finish: he knew the litany as well as anyone. "Like a whore's piss on a February morning: dirty, cold and yellow." He caught hold of Freddie's shoulder and steered him gently towards the landing. "Run along and chat with Mrs Taylor, there's a good lad." With any luck, Mrs Taylor would sequester Freddie in her kitchen and terrify him with a description of the spider veins along her nether parts.

* * *

"His throat's slit. The killer nearly took his head off." Freddie Collins straightened up, his mouth compressed so that it was nearly invisible. The police morgue was still cold at this hour; his breath steamed out in front of him.

"How long?" Devlin bent over the corpse, a handkerchief pressed against his nose and mouth. "I take it Abernathy had him removed to the morgue?"

"Yes, Sir. Couple of street arabs found him this morning, round about half past four."

Devlin removed the handkerchief long enough to grin.

"So that's why Old Brassie had you knocked up so early?" He didn't wait for Freddie's reply. "Judging by the smell, which I'm sure you've noticed, he's been dead a while." The man's face was puffed and bloated, the dead eyes starting from their sockets. The skin had darkened to a dusky greenish-grey. Like the previous victim, the hair had been set on fire, but beyond some slight singeing on the ends there was little damage. "This man has been dead four or five days," Devlin said. His mind started ticking like an overwound pocket watch. "Obviously whoever tried to burn his hair did so under wet conditions. The ends are only just burnt."

Devlin touched the ends of the man's hair and came away with some small, black particles clinging to his fingertips.

"Snuff?" Freddie asked.

"Absolutely not. See this?" Devlin dusted the particles on to a corner of the mortuary sheet. The fabric was none too clean (he made a mental jot to speak to someone), but the particles stood out nicely all the same. "These tiny bits of soot are burnt hair. When the hair burns freely, the ends tend to cling together and make bigger clumps. These pieces are very small." He waited while Freddie's mind worked over this particular fact.

"So this hair didn't burn freely," Freddie said.

"Yes."

"He was killed while he was wearing a hat?"

A part of Devlin hated to spoil Freddie's fun, nevertheless . . . "It was raining when the hair was set on fire. Hair doesn't burn as easily as you'd think. There are various dressing ointments and pomades, as well as the body's own natural oils.

You need ideal conditions, preferably outdoors in a dry location with the right amount of wind. Depending on what the
pomade is made of, it could slow down the fire or make the
hair burn faster." Devlin coughed in an offhanded manner.
"Did it rain last night?"

"Not last night . . . but last week it poured buckets,"
Freddie said. "Around Tuesday, I think. No, I'm a liar: it was
last Sunday."

Devlin seized upon this fact. "And today is . . . ?"

"Friday, Sir." A thought swam feebly across the surface of
Freddie's brain. "So the man we found in the alley . . ."

"The man in the alley wasn't the first victim. He was at
most the second victim, or probably the third, depending on
when Abernathy's body was killed."

"Inspector Abernathy's been killed?"

Devlin grimaced. "Would it were so." He flicked back the
sheet, his gaze roving freely over the dead man. "Collins, do
you know if there was a thumbprint?"

Freddie was silent.

"He's been washed, hasn't he?"

"Afraid so, Sir."

Devlin swore fluently.

"Cover him up." He gestured at the body, indicated that
Collins should follow him.

Devlin was already climbing the stairs and Collins, for all
his youth, was having difficulty keeping up. "Somebody
should tie you down," Freddie muttered. Despite the chill of
the morning and the necessary coldness of the police morgue,
he was sweating.

Back upstairs in Devlin's office, Freddie took himself off to make tea while Devlin tried to fit the pieces together. His skin had gone icy cold, but for all that, he was sweating as if he'd just run a mile behind a drover's cart.

Whittaker liked setting things on fire: when he and Devlin were still at school, he always carried a box of matches in his pocket and made a hobby of burning whatever he could lay his hands on. At chapel in the mornings he'd roll the pages of the hymnals and set them alight. In the evenings, when the other boys were busy with French verbs or bending over their copybooks, Whittaker occupied himself with the blankets on his bed. "The best thing to burn is hair," he once told Devlin. "It burns like anything." He didn't need to bother with his schoolwork: when he was old enough he'd inherit all his father's wealth and move out into Society. It was all he talked about, taking his place as the head of the family.

It must be terribly galling, Devlin thought, to have it taken away because of some carnal sport: the ravages of Whittaker's venereal disease would have necessarily barred him from Society for ever. Of course, none of this added up to a certainty; Whittaker was their best suspect, nothing more.

Devlin spent some time poring through files in the dusty storage room that was the final resting place of the Yard's voluminous archives. He found what he was looking for in some boxes toward the back, despite much sneezing and cursing and a painful wrench to his left elbow, caused when some bound volumes of *The Illustrated London News* fell on him.

I'm going to burn the little bitch. You see if I don't.

Devlin's head snapped up, every nerve taut and quivering. He could have sworn – no, his mind must be going. And anyway, there was no one here. He allowed himself the indulgence of a mental shrug and returned to burrowing through the boxes. Old Brassie didn't want Devlin on this case, which was why his lapdog Abernathy was all over it. Devlin was sweating, and not from any excess of heating in the archives room: his fingertips left several wet places on the papers he was sorting, and his collar was suddenly too tight. He reached to unbutton it, gave himself another mental shake. Damned room was giving him the willies.

He would never know why Whittaker had hesitated, or what had stayed his hand. Devlin had begged at the end, pleaded for his life, the knife blade against his throat while Whittaker grinned at him, his handsome face contorted by a monstrous glee. "I can kill you anytime, Phillip. Think I'll wait till later on, eh?"

Whittaker was a scion of a very old English family, obscure as his Saxon roots and just as bloody. He hadn't taken down any other tarts except Elizabeth Hobbs, and he'd pursued her across the length and breadth of London. Why? Perhaps Devlin's theory was correct and the girl was just a convenient target, or maybe it was sport, the urban equivalent of a rural foxhunt. Maybe Whittaker had run her to ground because he could, and maybe he'd taken his time doing it because he enjoyed it.

Devlin had been a stripling constable in those days, proud of the uniform and the fact that he was manly enough to fill it. He'd been assigned to the Complaints desk the first day she'd come in, just off the day shift at the woollen mills, smelling of lanolin and steam. Man chasing her, she said – she kept seeing him loitering in the street outside her lodgings. Did she ever take home gentlemen in the evenings? Devlin had phrased it to her as politely as he knew how, expecting that she would demur, protest that he was casting aspersions on her virtue, but no. She owned up to it, the brazen little doxy, said she often found a john or two amongst the toffs, who liked a bit on the side now and then. Especially a bit from down around the docks, a girl who knew all the proper tricks and still looked like she'd just come up to London from the country. Didn't give him no call to follow her around, she said, "interfere with" her. Devlin wondered where she'd got that phrase: certainly not in the woollen mills or on the streets.

The worst thing was her fragility, her wide blue eyes, her skin so pale as to be almost translucent. She seemed a thing made for light to pass through, wholly pure, and even then (though Devlin could not know it) she was in the tertiary stage of syphilis, dying by degrees.

Burn the little bitch. Oh yes, he remembered.

Devlin grasped the file tightly and willed the shaking in his hands to stop. There was nothing in the archive room to frighten him, nothing but his own imagination.

* * *

He had to admit he still liked watching Inspector Devlin. Especially now, when he was lying at the mercy of whatever he'd found in the archives, whatever sordid things were contained in the Yard's old files. Devlin in the midst of mental concentration was a sight to behold, with his collar button undone and his hair falling over his forehead, his long fingers twitching through the pages, oblivious to whatever might be lurking just beyond the door or even in the very room, for God's sake. For someone with as much experience as Devlin, such openly careless behaviour was practically an invitation to disaster, but Devlin was never what you'd call a mental giant. It was typical of the working classes: without the necessary background of good breeding, they retained a substandard intelligence, more suited to the clerical trades. Devlin would have done well as a shop assistant or a chemist. It wasn't like him, though, to let his guard down, to linger in a place like this alone without his faithful lapdog Collins by his side. One would think Devlin would understand the kinds of dangers that existed even in this place.

One would hope Devlin had not forgotten.

In the darkness of the archives room, John Whittaker permitted himself a tiny chuckle as he drew his gloves on.

CHAPTER THREE

FREDDIE COLLINS WAS waiting when Devlin returned from the archives, dusty but beaming in something very like triumph. "What time is it?" Devlin asked. He had a smudge of dirt on the tip of his nose and another on his chin. Freddie had to physically restrain himself from fetching out his handkerchief and cleaning the inspector up.

"Quarter to six." Freddie gestured at Devlin's face. "You seem to have collected a little evidence of your own, Sir."

"Eh?" Devlin gazed at him blankly, his mind still wholly occupied with the Whittaker files, the evidence and facts. He followed Freddie's pointing finger to the shaving mirror. "Damn." Devlin chuckled. "How is it you always notice such things, Constable?"

Freddie coughed diplomatically. "It's the light, Sir."

"Hmmm." Devlin was having trouble with his collar button, his fingers stiff with fatigue.

"Let me, Sir." Freddie's touch was rather more deft, but Freddie's hands weren't as cold as Devlin's, and Freddie hadn't been in that freezing archives room.

"How long have I been working here with you?" Freddie's hands had finished with the collar button and had somehow come to rest on Devlin's shoulders.

"Just a year, Collins, give or take. You were assigned to me almost as soon as you joined the Force."

Devlin smiled at the memory: a spit-shined Frederic Collins standing at attention in the doorway, his bowler underneath his arm, his gaze riveted on the wall behind Devlin's head. "They told me to come up, Sir."

"Have you ever known me to do anything exceptionally stupid?"

"Well, there was that one time with Lady Digby's parasol and that unfortunate small dog." Devlin let it go when he realised that Freddie wasn't laughing. "No," he said, "No, you've never done anything really stupid."

"Who taught me not to be stupid, eh? Who said to me, 'For the love of God, get your head down, don't be such a damned maniac'?"

Devlin smiled. "Constable, if you get anywhere near a point . . ."

The constable's hands tightened on Devlin's shoulders. "You're going to sit about and wait for him."

"Not wait," Devlin assured him. "No waiting required.

These corpses confirm it: John Whittaker is here in London." He grinned, and in his excitement swayed closer to the young constable, so close that their noses were all but touching.

"Oh, that eases my mind a lot, does that," Freddie murmured. He wouldn't have cared less, just then, if Whittaker had sailed in through the window and announced he was the Second Coming. Devlin was close to him: so close that Freddie could see the tiny flecks of gold in the inspector's dark, dark eyes, and the fine lines at their outer corners, and the indentation in Devlin's top lip.

"He's been setting them on fire." Devlin stepped away from Freddie, his mind whirling in an entirely new direction. "People are notoriously hard to burn."

"Burning people, Sir." Freddie tried to look intelligent. "I'll look into it, Sir."

Devlin ignored him. "Hair."

Freddie stared at him as if Devlin had grown extra limbs. "Again?" He had a horrible idea that Devlin might make him look at other burnt hair, on other dead bodies, or scrape the dead men's fingernails.

But Devlin was already quite in front of him, dashing around the desk, snatching up his coat and hat. Surely the library would have something, a chemistry text, some obscure work of reference. "Flames, man, flames! Bodies set on fire!" He called back over his shoulder to Freddie as the younger man struggled to keep up. "What if he's using some kind of fire starter? Something to make it burn."

"I don't understand," Freddie said. "You think Whittaker killed our body and the one Abernathy found. So that's two." The constable's forehead crinkled. "It's a bit tenuous. No disrespect intended, Sir, but aren't you stretching it a bit?"

"That'll do, Constable."

Whittaker had doused Elizabeth Hobbs in something, some chemical compound designed to make her burn. Any flammable liquid would do, anything to start the conflagration and keep it going. Once the subcutaneous fat had melted, the victim's clothing drew it up like a candle-wick, thus feeding the flames. Theoretically, a body burning in this manner could continue to do so for hours, but only under the right conditions. If the killer had used something, then perhaps that something had left a something else behind.

Within three days, Devlin had obtained samples of the eschar from every burned body presently in the morgue. He'd dispatched Freddie Collins to do the gathering, taking careful scrapings of the charred and ruined flesh and sealing each piece of vital evidence inside a test tube. It gave Freddie something useful to do and bolstered his belief in his own native intelligence, such as it was. Freddie unfortunately was so taken with this new procedure that he scraped every single body currently residing in the police morgue, including three old ladies who had expired in a house fire and the former Mr Azariah Blessed, rector of St Savior's Church, Seven Dials, and an unrepentant smoker. He had begun collecting hairs and clothing fibres when Devlin was forced to intervene: the police surgeon, never the most even-tempered of men, had begun making vague threats of physical violence involving a hat stand. Devlin went down and fetched Freddie back himself.

"But it's evidence," Freddie protested.

He laid a firm hand between Freddie's shoulder blades and propelled him up the stairs. "If you want to be useful, you can come to Fowler Street."

* * *

Devlin decided that there was no time like the present to educate young Collins about the strangeness of the pair he had dubbed the Resurrection Men. It would save much embarrassment later, when Freddie finally figured it out and allowed himself the luxury of a mental breakdown. "I don't feel that I need to tell you that Mr Harker and Mr Donnelly are rather . . . unconventional." That was putting it mildly, Devlin thought. "Neither is married and, although it's not widely known in Society, they have . . . well, an arrangement."

"What?" Freddie's mouth hung open artlessly. "You mean they're . . . perverts?"

"Not strictly an exclusive relationship, either. I've heard they have rather an open arrangement." Devlin coughed. "But you didn't hear it from me," and then there was nothing more to say, for their cab had arrived at its destination. Devlin led the way past Mrs Cadogan, who took their coats and bid them a good morning. On the landing just outside the Harker/Donnelly household, he took another moment to instruct Freddie about the "arrangement" between the two, so there would be no misunderstanding or unfortunate social gaffes. Freddie loved it when Devlin got like this, when he got all earnest and concerned, and his dark eyes shone and two spots of colour bloomed high up on each of the inspector's pale cheeks. Obviously Devlin liked giving lectures; it animated him as few things ever did.

"Inspector Devlin!" Harker, standing near the fireplace in one of his habitual poses, spun round with astonishing velocity and ushered Devlin and Collins into chairs. Harker was tall and hawk-like and perilously lean, with piercing pale-green eyes and an air of affected hauteur. "Donnelly has been called away for the morning, I fear – research in Kensington – so you have only my company to sustain you." He poured brandy for them both, despite the early hour, and offered them cigars, which Devlin refused and Collins accepted. Devlin sketched the outline of their problem for the solicitor, who sat with eyes tight shut in his favourite chair beside the fire. It was Harker's way to assume various poses and postures, the result of a lifetime spent among the upper classes (from whose unsuspecting loins he had sprung) and the scions of the Inner Temple. Harker was no longer practising the law, of course, having been summarily ejected from the bar after some shady dealings with the London underworld. Devlin didn't know the full details, but he'd heard that Harker had been caught in some sort of money-changing racket that involved a billiards table, three renters and a French poodle. Ever since his unfortunate tumble from the higher echelons, Harker had seen fit to content himself with a wayward residence among the opium dens and molly houses, with the occasional foray into chemical studies and some off-the-cuff "detective work". He was assisted in these affairs by his pet apothecary Donnelly, another ne'er-do-well who concerned himself with slightly recherché experiments on unwitting corpses, supposedly to aid Harker with his "detective work". Devlin thought better of wasting his breath in warnings: if Donnelly and Harker wanted to spend their leisure time invading graves, they deserved whatever they got. Not only had he bigger things to worry about than the Resurrection Men and their esoteric habits, but their interests occasionally proved useful to him.

"It is a thorny little problem, to be sure." Harker turned his pale green gaze on Collins and Devlin in turn.

"It is, Mr Harker." Devlin looked longingly at the cigar box next to Harker's elbow. "Er . . . may I?"

"You did have your chance, Devlin," Harker chided, but offered him the box anyway. "Go on, then."

Devlin accepted a light from the end of Collins's cigar and settled back in his chair. "I believe John Whittaker may have arrived in London, and I believe he may be responsible for at least two murders so far."

Harker's eyebrow rose to a dizzying height. "What is your rationale for such an astonishing pronouncement, Inspector?"

"The two bodies recently found had both been set on fire. One had a bloody thumbprint on the skin."

"And you suspect the murderer because . . .?"

"He was very careful about burning the hair. It's been done deliberately. You remember the Elizabeth Hobbs case?"

Harker's eyes flickered. "Young prostitute murdered and set on fire, yes. What has this to do with your current burn victims, Inspector?"

"Murder victims, Mr Harker, not burn victims, and I think Whittaker killed them."

"Indulge me, Inspector."

"Apart from the fact that both had their hair burned, nothing. I couldn't tell if the second body had the same thumbprint."

"Inspector Abernathy washed it," Freddie said.

"All on his own?" Harker asked, bitchily. "I'm astonished. I have seen Inspector Abernathy and I'm amazed he can fasten his sleeve links without outside intervention."

"This is merely instinct on my part, Mr Harker." It was true, and it was precious little to go on. "Whittaker was – is – syphilitic. He claimed to have been infected by Elizabeth Hobbs. But what if she was merely convenient?"

"In what way?" Harker topped up their glasses from the decanter.

"Convenient because she's a woman and thus an effective alibi for Whittaker. What if Whittaker contracted syphilis through someone else? When I saw her, she was supposedly in the tertiary stages and should have been in hospital."

"Yet she continued to work in the woollen mills and on the streets, so she could hardly have been at death's door. If Donnelly were here he would tell you that a tertiary syphilitic could not possibly infect another. Perhaps she was blackmailing him. Who else would Whittaker have gotten syphilis from?"

"A man." Devlin took a sip of his brandy, relishing the slow warmth as it went down. "Why do you think Whittaker Senior disinherited his son? Surely, Mr Harker, you can understand it: John Whittaker was primed and ready to take over the family seat."

"So," Harker said, "the father disinherits the son because young Whittaker is an invert."

"Whittaker wanted nothing more than his rightful entry into Society. When his father found out his son's true nature, he put a stop to it, disinherited him and bestowed the bulk of the estate on some female relative."

"Progressive," Harker mused. "The bluestockings must have adored him."

"After he was disinherited, Whittaker dropped out of sight for a few years," Devlin said.

Harker asked. "And what was he doing during his prolonged absence?"

Devlin rubbed his hands together; he was warming to this theory. "At first I thought he'd died or something, but then he resurfaced. He was living with a renter in a lodging house near Covent Garden. Surely you've heard of William Osborne? Spanish William, they call him. But William isn't syphilitic, so I can't think what they were doing together. William got out when Whittaker started knocking him about, but Whittaker always did like it rough. No doubt he went right out and found himself a stevedore, just to take the edge off."

"How do you know this?" Freddie's voice was low, tense. Both Devlin and Harker turned to look at him. "How do you know so much about what he's like?" The constable's arms were crossed over his chest; he was holding on to his elbows, hugging himself.

"We were at school together," Devlin said. Not the whole truth, but it would have to do, and he wasn't about to give

Freddie an illustrated history. "I got hold of Spanish William, brought him in to the Yard for a chat."

Harker got up and went over to the fireplace, tossed another log in and poked it. A bright shower of sparks flew up, the light illuminating their faces for a moment. Harker looked interested and Devlin clearly animated, while Freddie just looked blank. No, not blank, Devlin thought, hollow, as though someone had reached in and taken his insides out. The deepening gloom threw the lower half of his body into shadow, vanished him away.

"So Whittaker was angry," Harker said, "and he wanted to get his own back. He couldn't kill off his father, because he'd never get within six feet of the old man. The sister? She'd married a soldier and followed him to India, no help there."

"Whittaker wouldn't go to India," Devlin said, "he's too damned lazy. Constable, are you quite all right?"

"I'm going outside," Freddie said. "I think I'll smoke a cigarette out on the pavement."

Harker exchanged a look with Devlin. "You may smoke in here, Constable."

"No." Freddie got up, moved to the door without looking at either of them; both men heard his footsteps on the stairs.

"He . . . he doesn't know," Devlin said. A great silence had descended between Harker and himself.

"Perhaps you ought to tell him," Harker replied. He gazed at Devlin, not unkindly. "Would it be so bad?"

"London," Devlin continued as though Harker hadn't spoken at all, "is overrun with whores, and no one cares if one of them is murdered. There was a panic during the Ripper murders because people were afraid he might come after them." Devlin tossed his cigar into the fireplace. What the devil was Freddie doing outside? Why didn't he come back into the house? "These latest victims are Whittaker's, Mr Harker. He burned Elizabeth Hobbs and left a bloody thumbprint on her thigh. The murdered man we found in the alley? The same thing. The hair had been set on fire and he had a thumbprint in the middle of his chest."

"This could be someone copying Whittaker," Harker pointed out, and, "Inspector, do stop worrying about your constable. Young Collins will come to no harm outside."

"Couldn't be," Devlin replied, "because no one outside of Scotland Yard even knew about the thumbprint he left on the girl."

"Are you certain of that, Inspector?"

"As certain as I can be, yes. The only other person who might have known would be the police surgeon in charge of the morgue, and he died several years after the Hobbs case. We've got a new surgeon now, new morgue attendants, the whole bit."

"Hmmm." Harker thought for a moment. "If this murderer of yours has access to some unusual kind of chemical – say, eau de toilette, for example – then he would tend to use it again and again. Whatever is easiest to lay the hands upon." Harker sucked at his cigar and fell into a brown study, a pose that borrowed liberally from *The Strand* magazine. "What must be established, my dear Devlin, is this: the residues left behind by various chemicals can differ from one another widely, or be frustratingly similar. If your murderer took care to use something which leaves its own unique chemical signature, so much the better for us. Certain chemicals react with certain other chemicals, as I am sure you know. I myself have developed a number of different chemical tests to determine the presence of such compounds." Harker examined his fingernails. "Not that the scientific press care about such things. I am merely a footnote to history, Inspector."

"Er, yes, of course." Footnote to history?

"If that easily detected signature appears in several of the bodies that have so lately passed through the police morgue, again, it is to our benefit, because we have a circumstantial linkage. What we are looking for is an esoteric or unusual compound, something which he used as a means of inciting the conflagration, but which leaves behind a traceable residue when it is burned. To find such a chemical would be luck indeed, Inspector."

Devlin waited patiently for Harker to continue, but the solicitor seemed to be sunk in his own musings. "And?"

"Leave the samples with me. This is a problem for science, Devlin, and I daresay you have other lines of inquiry to follow?"

"Yes, of course." Mundane things, the everyday detritus of city life, nothing as interesting or potentially as chilling as this. There was a motion at the door and Freddie appeared, smelling like tobacco smoke and cold air.

"Bloody cold outside," Freddie said.

Harker rose grandly, indicating that the interview was at an end. "Thank you, gentlemen. I shall be in touch." He reached into the pocket of his dressing gown and brought forth a blank piece of paper, approximately the size of a matchbox cover. "My card."

"Mr Harker," Freddie turned. "You wouldn't be familiar with a pub called the Peacock Club? I'm certain I saw you there."

"Ah, Constable, there you have me. I have truck with neither peacocks nor the clubs in which they habitually congregate." Harker offered them a chilly smile. "Good day, gentlemen."

As Devlin took Freddie out on to the landing, Harker could be heard bellowing at Mrs Cadogan for hot water. "What Peacock Club?" Devlin demanded, collaring Freddie at the first turning of the stairs. "What in God's name got into you?"

Freddie shrugged. "Sorry, Sir. Must've forgot myself."

"And another thing . . ." Devlin was winding up for the full speech when Freddie interrupted him.

"What day's this, Sir?"

Devlin stared at him. "What day? You mean, day of the week?"

"Day of the week, Sir."

"It's Friday." He stared at Collins. "Why?"

"You know what tomorrow is, Sir."

"Saturday?"

"Mrs Alcock's tea dance, Sir. You asked me to remind you, Sir."

"When did I ask you to remind me?"

Freddie had the good grace to fidget. "Not in so many

words, Inspector . . . but it was written on your blotter. Tea dance, Old Brassie, Saturday eight o'clock, it said." He huffed out an impatient breath. "You're always after me to notice things."

Devlin paused on Mrs Cadogan's final landing and rammed his forehead against the wall. Of course he had forgotten. Of course he had to go. And he had to take Freddie with him. He'd bloody well take Freddie with him, now. "I think you should attend as well, Constable." Devlin tried to keep from grinning as he stepped outside, breathing deep of the bracing October air. "You can keep an eye on the silver."

Devlin hailed a cab and climbed aboard.

"Me?" Freddie's neck made several contractions, not unlike a dodgy ostrich. "What for?"

Devlin sat back and smiled, reached out to clap Freddie briskly on the arm. "I do believe his Phoebe's looking for a husband," he said.

The look on Constable Collins's face amused Devlin all the way back to Scotland Yard.

* * *

Sir Neville Alcock was waiting when Devlin got back; he barely had time to get his coat off before he was summoned. He found Alcock with George Abernathy at his side. The sight of Abernathy gave him even more of a sinking feeling than usual.

Alcock didn't even let him get the usual pleasantries (feigned as they were) out of the way. "Devlin, take a look at this," he said. Abernathy was holding what appeared to be a

woman's hatbox; it was curiously decorated with myriad pur-
plish dapples and swatches.

"I'll stick with my bowler if nobody minds," Devlin said.
Neither Alcock nor Abernathy laughed.

"This arrived at the front desk by messenger twenty minutes ago." Abernathy laid the hatbox down on the desk and
opened it. Devlin realised that the blotches on the box were
blood. It contained a human head.

"Don't recognise him," Devlin said smoothly. "Must be
one of Abernathy's relatives." His insides were squirming
with horror, but he'd be damned if he'd let Abernathy see it.
"Who is he?"

"He's no one," Alcock said. "An antiquated renter. Name
of Charles Darwin. His friends called him Chimpy."

"I'll just bet they did," Devlin mused.

"He was last seen soliciting business in Bethnal Green,"
Abernathy said. "Simian-looking bugger, isn't he?"

"This was addressed to you,"

Abernathy wasn't quite smirking. "It's your case now,
Phillip. You can have it. You've done your best to cut me out
at every turn. Keep the bloody head if you like." His fat face
shone with moisture.

"That'll do." Alcock swung his stomach around the desk.
"Devlin, the head was addressed to you. I've sent the note up
to your office. Young Collins is taking down the details. Better stay late this evening. I expect you'll want to fiddle about
and do whatever it is that you do."

For a few horrifying moments Devlin thought Sir Neville
was making some lewd reference to Collins and himself. "Of

course, Sir." He peered into the hatbox. "What about him?"

"You're welcome to take it down to the morgue." Alcock gestured to Abernathy, who was still holding the hat box. "Give him the head, George." Abernathy handed it over; it was heavier than Devlin expected, but he wasn't used to carting human heads about the premises.

"And the rest of him?" Devlin fumbled with the hatbox lid.

"We never found the rest of him," Abernathy said.

"You mean *you* never found the rest of him," Devlin remarked. "How unsurprising."

"Run along, Inspector Abernathy," Alcock said. "I'll catch you up later for a brandy." He waited till Abernathy had left. "Very nasty business, Devlin."

"Abernathy is a bloody idiot," Devlin said. The head was slipping; he held the box more tightly, careful not to smear the blood.

"Yes." Alcock collapsed into his chair with a gusty sigh. "What sort of man wants to receive a human head?"

"Abernathy, apparently, since he seems to be in the habit of opening my mail." Devlin rested the box on Alcock's desk.

"The murderer has taken a shine to you, Devlin."

"With respect, Sir, I don't think so. Quite the opposite, in fact. This sort of thing is usually meant as an insult."

"Or a message." Alcock harrumphed in a self-important fashion. "Find this bastard and bring him in. Get this sorted."

"Yes, Sir." He gathered the head into his arms.

"You're dismissed, Devlin." Alcock flapped one fat hand at him. "Go away."

* * *

The police morgue, despite its inherent cheerlessness, was one of Devlin's favourite places. For one thing, it was quiet, and the occupants did a fair sight less complaining than those in the rest of the building. For another, it occasionally hosted one Nigel Pence, a promising young medical student and the resident laboratory enthusiast. It was Pence who took Devlin's bizarre samples and examined them seriously, and quite often it was Pence who found precisely what Devlin suspected might be there. "Missed me, did you?" Pence came round the end of the table. He was shorter than Devlin and slight, with longish brown hair and round spectacles. "I've been talking to Molly here." He indicated the corpse of an elderly woman. "Gave her a lovely wash and all."

"I bet she loved that," Devlin replied. He laid the hatbox down next to the old woman's feet. "I've got something special for you."

"And yet you brought your burned bits to Reggie Harker," Pence sighed. "Making idle time with the Resurrection Men?"

"From what I've heard, Reggie Harker keeps chaps like you supplied with corpses." Devlin cast a quick look over the morgue. "Or he used to." He canted a look at Pence. "Doing your own burking these days?"

Pence held up a hand. "I would never desecrate the dead," he said reverently.

"Harker is the best man as far as chemistry goes, and you know it. Besides, I'd never trust Harker with the sorts of things I bring you." Fingernails and teeth and hair and pieces of bloodied cloth: Pence examined everything that Devlin brought to him, made sense of it and understood why Devlin collected the kinds of evidence he did.

"You're a hundred years ahead of your time, Inspector."

Not many people understood how a single fleck of paint on a dead man's fingernail could lead Devlin back to a metal manufacturer in Stepney, or the way a torn scrap of bloodied petticoat might reveal the profession of its owner. Devlin noticed things that others overlooked; sometimes the things he noticed helped him solve a case and sometimes not.

"Sir Neville thinks you'd like to see this." Devlin opened up the hatbox.

"Ooooh," Pence sighed happily. "Is he yours? Can I play with him?"

"Dead renter," Devlin told him. "The murderer is an old friend of mine. The head was sent to me as a parcel."

"Any note with it?" Pence asked. "Flowers, sweetmeats, silk undergarments?" He lifted the head out of the box. "Hello, darling."

"His name's Charles Darwin. Not *the* Charles Darwin, mind you. His friends called him Chimpy." Devlin glanced at the young man. "Shall I just leave it here?"

"Right." Pence tore himself away from his contemplation of the head. "Do you know how difficult it is to find a complete, intact human head? With the brain contents and everything?"

"You'll tell me something about Chimpy in a little while?"

"Oh, yes, Inspector. Cause of death and all that. You'll get a full report."

Devlin found Freddie sitting at the desk – Devlin's desk – and staring down at a sheet of paper. "You all right?" Devlin asked. He had never seen Freddie so absorbed, unless food was involved.

"I've never seen paper like this," Freddie said. He stood up and let Devlin sit down.

"Fancy, is it?" Devlin held the sheet up to the light. The note was written on heavy cream paper with the watermark of an exclusive West End stationer. "Hmmm, very posh indeed." He didn't recognise the handwriting. It wasn't Whittaker's, at least the way he remembered it, but that could mean anything or nothing. Whittaker could have deliberately altered his handwriting. If he were truly syphilitic, then the disease could have affected the steadiness of his arm, although the writing didn't appear shaky or ill-coordinated.

"Maybe he got someone else to write it." Freddie peered over Devlin's shoulder.

"Like who?"

The constable shrugged. "A confederate, someone working with him, someone he can trust." Freddie slipped into his overcoat. "If you're not needing me, Sir, I thought I'd finish up for the day."

"What?" Devlin was still occupied with the note. "What time is it?"

"Just gone half-six, Sir." Freddie knotted a thick muffler round his throat. "Are you staying late?"

The handwriting appeared to be left-handed, and Devlin

knew Whittaker was right-handed. But the writing didn't have the awkwardness he'd have expected from a false script.

"You should go home, Sir." Freddie was gazing down at him with a curious expression of tenderness and concern. "It's late. You've not eaten hardly all day."

"I'm fine, Constable. That'll be all." Damn it, why did Freddie keep pushing?

He was talking to himself; the constable had already left. Devlin turned his attention back to the note.

Chapter Four

I T WAS AS bad as Devlin had expected. No, it was worse, for there was absolutely no liquor to be had, just Mrs Alcock's putrid punch and the ever-present pots of tea. Devlin had poured himself a glass of punch and carried it held out slightly in front of him, as if to fend off any eligible women with fantasies of marriage. He wished bitterly that he'd thought to bring his silver brandy flask – a few dollops of that and even Mrs Alcock's punch might be remotely palatable.

"You must be Inspector Devlin."

He turned rather more quickly than he ought, sloshing punch out of the glass and on to his shoes. He found he was looking at a woman perhaps his own age, wearing a stunning evening dress in navy blue; her face was a perfect rounded oval, smooth as milk, and her eyes were somewhere between brown and green. "I'm afraid you have the advantage of me, Miss . . .?"

"Oh, forget that nonsense." She stuck her hand into his and shook it with a surprisingly strong grip. "I'm Phoebe Alcock. I bet Father invited you here because he's trying to marry me off. Am I right?"

"Something like that."

She grinned, revealing two rows of perfect white teeth. "Well, don't worry. I've no intention of burdening you with anything like that. I deplore these tea dances of Mother's. You'd think she'd know by now."

"You're not interested in marriage?" She was the first one yet, Devlin thought. He was certain English females had the nesting instinct infused into their brains at birth, by some sort of magical syringe.

"Marriage?" Phoebe's pretty face assumed a shocked expression. "Are you mad?" She laughed uproariously, her small, plump hands latticed across her lovely mouth. "Not bloody likely." She leaned close to Devlin and spoke confidentially. "Have you got a fag? I'm dying for a puff." She reached into Devlin's silver cigarette case and extracted one, toyed with it for a moment or two. "I can't smoke it in here – Mother would have a fit. Come out into the arbour with me. We can talk." And she took his arm and steered him after her.

It was a warm evening for October, as evidenced by the many doors and windows of Sir Neville's house that were left

wide open to the breeze. Phoebe led him up a small incline
to a gazebo, set behind a stand of poplar trees, out of direct
sight of the house.

"You know Freddie Collins is absolutely mad about you,"
she began. Devlin struck a match to hide his incipient confusion, held it carefully to light her cigarette. "He tries to
make out like he isn't, but anybody with eyes can see he'd be
on you in a minute." She tilted her head and gazed at Devlin.
"You're not used to a woman talking this way, are you?"

Devlin conceded that he was not.

"Mother sent me to America to be educated – I suppose
it's made me rather sharper with my tongue than I would be
otherwise." She slanted a gaze at him. "You're awfully handsome – how come you're not married?"

"Ah . . . well, you see, I'm very busy and police work –"

"You're going to tell me that a policeman's life is no life for
the wife and kiddies, and you wouldn't want to tie yourself to
home and hearth while there are criminals afoot." She laughed
gently. "I've heard it all before, Inspector. And yet to look at
you –" She trailed off abruptly. "I think I've said too much."

But Devlin was curious to hear the rest. She had a way
about her, and it intrigued him. "Please – go on."

Phoebe took a long drag on her cigarette, exhaled smoke
with a practised air. "You're a lovely man, Inspector," she said
softly, "but you have the loneliest eyes I've ever seen. You're
scared to death to let someone close to you. You think you'd
be compromising yourself if you did. Losing that keen edge
of yours." She shook her head, crushed the cigarette under
the heel of her dancing slipper.

Devlin was silent for a long moment. "I wish there was something else to drink besides that awful punch," he blurted, and could have bitten off his tongue.

In a trice, Phoebe reached into her reticule and handed him a silver flask. "Brandy," she explained. "Mother makes the punch and I can't stand the bloody stuff. I've been tippling ever since this damned thing started."

* * *

Devlin couldn't remember when he'd been this drunk – whatever Phoebe Alcock had put into her little flask, it bloody well wasn't brandy, or at least, it wasn't any brandy that he had ever had. "They're going to wonder where we are, inside the house," he slurred. For some long moments he had been discoursing with Phoebe on the nature of humanity, and whether it was possible for anyone to be entirely good. Phoebe told him that she had absolutely no desire to be good, that it was better to be interesting.

"How long have we been out here?" Devlin wondered if Phoebe even had a watch.

She did. "It's nearly midnight," she said. "We've been out here the whole time."

"Your father is going to kill me." Devlin rested his head in his hands and closed his eyes. The gazebo seemed to be mounted on wheels and was spinning about him like Mr Ferris's famous carnival ride.

Phoebe gazed at him thoughtfully. "Do you know that Freddie Collins is in love with you?"

Devlin stared at her. "I don't think he is."

"Why?" Phoebe reached out, laid her palm against his cheek. He was such a dear thing, lonely and unutterably sad, and so bloody fragile in his own way.

"He never said." Devlin nodded with the weighty sagacity of the thoroughly drunk.

Phoebe studied him for a moment. "Would you?" she asked quietly. "Oh, it's not the way it used to be, Inspector. A hundred years ago, not even that – Byron and Shelley and Keats – it was an elevated thing, like Alexander the Great."

Devlin blinked. "Keats was a pouf?" He was quite confused. "Are we even talking about the same thing? I should think that you . . ."

The rest of it died in his throat, unspoken, as she reached for him and kissed him tenderly, a tenderness that was curiously without passion.

"I'm sorry." She released him. "I don't know why I did that." She slipped away from him, moving through the darkness towards the house.

"Sir?" Freddie Collins's face filled the whole of Devlin's vision. "Are you . . ." He drew back in astonishment, then began to laugh. "You're drunk!"

"Sh– shut it." Devlin tried to loop an arm around Collins's neck and thus steady himself, but was unable to make his limbs obey him. "No need to tell . . ." He waved expansively at the house, including the grounds and all the occupants. ". . . everyone."

Freddie wrapped his arm around Devlin's slim waist, steadying him. "I think I ought to take you home, Inspector." He walked Devlin carefully down the gazebo steps and into the cool night air. "You're in no condition to be going about on your own."

"What if Whittaker comes back?" Devlin fought to make his eyes focus.

"Whittaker?" Freddie felt the hot flush of anger in his face and fought it back. "I'll thrash him from here to Kingdom Come!" He moved Devlin the short distance down the gravel drive to where a four-wheeler was waiting, handed the inspector inside and got in beside him. "I won't let Whittaker anywhere near you." He wondered when he'd become so voluble in his devotion.

"Phoebe said . . ." But Devlin thought better of it. He closed his eyes and seemed asleep in moments.

Freddie Collins reached across the dark confines of the carriage, patted Devlin familiarly and took the inspector into his arms.

* * *

Devlin awoke groaning, in an unfamiliar bed and an unfamiliar set of circumstances. His head felt at least as large as Sir Neville's belly, but not nearly so soft or padded. And he wasn't alone: through weighted eyes he peered at the blond head on the pillow next to his. Freddie bloody Collins! Devlin reached out gingerly and rapped his knuckles against the constable's forehead. "Wake up!" he snapped, and regretted it instantly. The volume seemed to be causing the insides of his head to slosh about in a most disagreeable manner, and his stomach seemed to be rising to meet the unfortunate condition of his brains. He fairly bolted from the bed and was halfway to the closet of ease when it occurred to him that he was absolutely mother-naked. This was the last coherent thought he was to have for some long moments, for all his energies were spent in expelling the contents of his stomach.

Dimly, he heard Freddie speaking behind him and reached out an arm to wave him away. It was all bloody bad enough – here his thoughts were curtailed by another wave of vomiting – bloody bad enough to be upchucking into Freddie Collins's facilities, but even worse to be doing it without a shred of dignity. How in God's name could he explain himself, or even look the constable squarely in the eye?

He sat back on his heels, his ribs and abdomen sore from this most recent bout. A hand appeared within his field of vision and passed him a cold cloth, which Devlin took gratefully and applied to his sweating forehead. "What?" The taste of bile had backed up into his throat, and he pressed his eyes closed against another rising wave of nausea. "Where is this?"

"Let me get you sorted, Guv'nor." Freddie reached out to help him to his feet, but Devlin struck out savagely. "Oi! There's no call for that, Sir."

But Devlin, his mind elsewhere, didn't bother to reply. His hand had found a towel on the rack near by, and he wrapped it around his middle in the manner of a Polynesian warlord.

Devlin staggered against the washbasin and nearly fell. He ground his teeth together in frustration and pain; it felt as if his eyeballs were going to pop out. "Where are my clothes?"

"I hung 'em up for you – keep the wrinkles out." Freddie indicated the wardrobe just beyond, its door standing open,

Devlin's clothing clearly visible. Devlin pushed past the younger officer and seized his trousers, yanked them on over the towel.

"Haven't got time for this," Freddie heard him say. "Bloody tea dance at bloody Brassie's house then bloody drinking with his bloody daughter and her bloody brandy."

Devlin rammed his feet into his shoes and cast about the room for his hat and overcoat. "And what use were you last night, eh? Left me on my own with that spinster and her witches' brew. Rubbing elbows with the toffs, were you?"

This was unfair, and both Freddie and Devlin knew it. From another man, Freddie Collins would never countenance such an attack, and on a reasonable day, he wouldn't countenance it from Devlin, either. But he knew Devlin was horribly hungover and doubtless feeling as if he had been crushed under the wheels of a costermonger's cart.

"I'm going," Devlin said savagely, "and don't follow me!"

The door slammed shut behind him, and Freddie was alone. He allowed himself a philosophic gesture, in the form of screwing his eyes shut and twitching at his neat moustache violently with his index finger. He sighed gustily once or twice, went back into the lavatory and stared at himself in the mirror. "You're a bloody idiot, you." His mouth compressed itself into a line underneath the neat moustache. "Stripping all his clothes off. Did you think he weren't going to notice?"

* * *

Devlin spent the rest of Sunday subsisting on chicken broth and weak tea and waiting for his heaving guts to subside.

By the time he left his rooms on Monday, the whole city was humming with the news about the bodies. George Abernathy had been talking to a journalist from the Central Press Syndicate, and now a drawing of Abernathy's version of things was featured on the pages of just about every newspaper in London. Alcock had said he wanted it kept quiet, Devlin thought sourly, but obviously such discretion didn't extend to his favourite, Abernathy. No, Abernathy could probably drop his drawers in the middle of his master's office and get nothing for it but a thank-you. CORPSES IN THE STREETS: YARD MAN SAYS WORST YET TO COME. Had Alcock authorised this? What in God's name was he thinking? Or Alcock hadn't authorised it and Abernathy was acting on his own accord, and likely to catch hell for it later on. Probably he figured that being Alcock's golden boy would save him from the boss's wrath. Devlin made a mental note to be there when Alcock put Abernathy out a window.

Devlin had arisen early this morning and treated himself to a shave and haircut at Windigger's barbershop. Normally he shaved himself, but the events of the past few days and the reappearance of Whittaker had convinced him that he deserved a little treat, even if Windigger's rates were exorbitant and Devlin could hardly afford it on a policeman's salary. He would be the last man to think of himself as being niggardly over money, but his colleagues at the Yard made a point of routinely inspecting the seat of his trousers to ascertain the degree of wear.

He slipped into the chair, submitted himself to Windigger's tender ministrations and was massaged, clipped, pummelled, soaped, scraped and had his cheeks pinched into what, for Devlin, passed for glowing health. Make no mistake: Devlin hadn't yet found a barber to surpass or even equal Windigger, an elderly Dutchman with a surfeit of nose and ear hair, and the halitosis of a week-dead corpse.

"I heard about your troubles. Terrible, terrible. The newspaper says that Scotland Yard can do nothing!" He dropped this into one of Devlin's ears as his scissors did their work.

"I've no idea where you got that idea, Mr Windigger." Devlin felt a knot of anger growing underneath his breastbone: why couldn't bloody Abernathy keep his big mouth shut? "Never heard such silliness in my life."

"But they say that even now there are corpses piling up in the streets."

"Rubbish." Devlin bit back a sigh. "Look, how much longer is this going to take? I've to be at the Yard in half an hour."

Windigger took his scissors away and twirled Devlin's chair – and Devlin himself – like a carousel. "There. You are handsome, Inspector."

"Humph." Devlin grumbled at his own reflection in the mirror opposite, wondering when he'd achieved those dark rings underneath his eyes.

"But a little tired-looking, if I might say."

"Mind your own business!" Devlin snapped.

He slipped into his coat and gathered his gloves; the October morning was sunny and bright, but held that unmistakable breath of winter. "Don't believe everything you read in the papers." He pressed a shilling into Windigger's outstretched hand. "And thank you."

He decided to walk the moderate distance to the Yard, to get some fresh air and also to delay the inevitable meeting with Freddie Collins. Just this once, Devlin wished that Freddie could be elsewhere, for he was still curiously amnesiac about events immediately following Old Brassie's tea dance and embarrassed that he had evidently turned up in the bed of his subordinate completely au natural. Of course, Freddie's reasoning in the matter had been perfectly sound: Devlin would have been considerably put out if he had awakened to find he'd slept in his clothing. Still, that didn't warrant being stripped to the skin and deposited into bed beside a man who was in a similar state of undress. Perhaps Freddie merely thought he was doing Devlin a favour and meant nothing by it. Why was Freddie always looking at him with his great moon eyes? Here Devlin grumbled again, stepped neatly around a steaming pile of horse turds and on to the pavement opposite. Freddie hadn't – as far as Devlin could tell – so much as laid a finger on him. Freddie had been absolutely circumspect in every regard.

For some reason this made Devlin incredibly depressed.

He reached his desk a little after nine, having successfully dodged Sir Neville Alcock, who was deep in heated conversation with three sergeants near the lift. He wondered how much, if anything, Phoebe had said to her father about Devlin's questionable conduct at the dance. He hoped to God she was intelligent enough to understand that even an intimation of inappropriate behaviour would be sufficient to ensure that Devlin's stones became a permanent fixture in Sir Neville's office, alongside the elephant foot rubbish bin and the monkey paw ashtray. He shuddered to think of his bollocks floating in ether at Sir Neville's meaty elbow.

There was a cup of tea waiting for him, and Freddie Collins appeared, all graciousness and good intentions, to take Devlin's coat and hat. If the constable was still upset about Devlin's behaviour to him on Sunday, he made no mention of it now, but Devlin could detect the pungent stench of hurt feelings a mile off. Freddie was particularly obsequious this morning, which immediately put Devlin on the defensive: every time Devlin so much as looked at Freddie, the constable flinched, until Devlin believed himself capable of any number of heinous acts.

"See here, Constable."

"There's a message for you as well, Sir, from Nigel Pence, and shall I freshen up your tea?" Freddie's gaze rested somewhere around the knot of Devlin's tie and moved no higher.

"Collins."

"I expect Nigel wants to see you, Sir. Probably something to do with the note. Or the head." Here the constable bit his bottom lip and fell into a grievous brown study that rendered him very nearly catatonic. So intent was he upon his private mourning that he completely missed Devlin's immediate directive.

"Sir?"

"I said, shut the bloody door!" Devlin got up from his desk, but Freddie was quicker and closed the door of Devlin's office with a punctilious "click" that would not have been out of place at the Prussian royal court. He then adopted an attitude of profound humility and stared at the floor between Devlin's feet.

"Out with it." Devlin leaned against his desk and crossed his arms on his chest. "Come on. Let's get this bloody air cleared before we both smother."

The constable raised his eyes and looked Devlin full in the face. "I wanted to tell you . . . that is . . . well, see here, Sir . . ." At this point words failed him, and he appealed to Devlin mutely, his warm brown eyes overbrimmed with misery.

Devlin sighed. There was no way in God's name that he could even think to broach a subject as delicate as this with Freddie looking as if Devlin had just murdered his kitten. "Saturday night," he said finally. He'd had it all planned out, what he'd been going to say, even down to his facial expressions and the placement of his feet. Right now, his feet were betraying the rest of him by creeping ever so slowly towards Freddie Collins, until finally Devlin was gazing into the constable's eyes. "Thank you for taking care of me." He laughed self-consciously and rubbed a thumb across his eyebrow. "Made a bloody fool of myself, I did." Devlin straightened his shoulders and tried to look authoritative, even though his stomach was attempting just then to invert itself entirely and come out his windpipe. "And that scene first thing on Sunday . . . well."

Freddie smiled gently. "I see you've been to the barber this morning," he said.

"What?"

"Windigger, isn't it?"

Devlin blinked at him like a startled animal. "Yes, I always go to Windigger."

"And he always cuts you in the very same spot."

"Cuts me?"

"When he shaves you, he always gets you right there."

Devlin's hand explored the contours of his naked face. "Where?"

"Right here." Freddie's fingers ghosted against his cheek, a whispered touch, no more, but Devlin jerked away as though he'd been burned; Freddie pretended not to notice. "And there's a telegram."

"Who's the telegram from?" Freddie oughtn't stand so close: it did strange things to him, it might be misconstrued. A policeman must always be above reproach; he knew that.

"Reginald Harker." Freddie read out the message: "NOTHING UNUSUAL STOP AMBERGRIS MAIN INGREDIENT STOP NO PRECISE CONCLUSIONS STOP."

Devlin sank into his chair and buried his chin in his hands, dimly aware that the hard surface of his desk was exerting an uncomfortable pressure on his elbows. "Damn!" He took the telegram from Freddie.

"It's the law of averages," he said. "For everything of significance you find, you are just as likely to find nothing at all."

"But this ambergris . . ." Freddie began uncertainly. "If the murderer uses cologne to set their hair on fire . . ."

"Go on."

"If he uses cologne to set their hair on fire, and if that cologne contains this whale vomit rubbish that Mr Harker and Mr Pence both think it does, and if Whittaker is our main suspect, then mightn't we be able to find out where Whittaker buys his cologne, and if that cologne contains amber-whatsit, then we've got a link tying Whittaker to the crimes." Suddenly devoid of breath after that mammoth utterance, Freddie visibly deflated and lapsed into silence.

Devlin nodded. "Most people buy things wherever it's convenient." He gnawed on his bottom lip. "And most murderers stick to their own neighbourhoods." Devlin hauled out a map and spread it open on the desk. "Our murderer has, so far as we know," he slurped at his tea, "killed two or perhaps three men."

"That we know of." Freddie reached around Devlin with the teapot and decanted a stream of the hot brew into Devlin's cup.

"That we know of." Devlin traced a circle on the map in front of him. "These bodies have all been discovered in the East End, in the very same area frequented by Jack the Ripper. The first man we found here, in spitting distance of the Ten Bells pub." He marked an X in pencil.

"Right. And that other chap was just off Mitre Square."

"Again, another location much in favour with the Ripper." Devlin put another X on the map.

Devlin thought for a moment. "I've got a job for you."

"For me?" Collins was still holding the teapot.

Devlin circled the area on the map. "I want you to have a little look round for me. Do a thorough sweep of apothecaries, chemists, anyone who might make up perfumes and colognes, especially expensive perfumes and colognes. Ask them about any repeat customers, and ask them if there's anyone who has bought a large amount of the stuff." Devlin gave him the map. "Do you understand?"

"Yes, Sir." Freddie slipped into his overcoat and stowed the map in his pocket. "Fancy cologne and lots of it, Sir."

"Precisely. I'm going down to have a talk with Mr Pence."

"Is it about the head, Sir?"

"It is." He handed Freddie his muffler. "Good luck, Constable. And good hunting."

Devlin descended into the bowels of Scotland Yard and found Nigel Pence staring fixedly at the head; two days of inattention in the morgue had not improved the smell. "I got your note," Devlin said. "You've found something?"

"Do you know, Inspector, it's so very difficult to get good specimens these days. For medical study, I mean. And one can only do so many dissections of pigs and sheep and, Lord love us, Sir, horses. It's not the same thing." Pence gave Devlin a magnifying glass. "Have a look at his ears."

"His ears?" Devlin did as he was told, examining first one and then the other. "What am I looking for, Mr Pence?" The smell was quite nauseating, and Devlin couldn't quite get used to Chimpy's opaque stare. He knew it was the post-mortem degradation of the cells in the eye, but it looked like his Uncle Jeremiah's cataracts. Uncle Jeremiah, who smelled like rotten socks and gin and who farted at the dinner table.

"You probably wouldn't notice," Pence replied, in a tone that was just this side of condescending, "being a layman and all. The eardrum on the right is quite thoroughly punctured."

"Is it?" So the dead renter was deaf on one side, how very sad for him.

"Not only punctured, but by something slender and cylindrical."

"Ah." Devlin felt his eyebrows rise. "And were you able to recover this slender, cylindrical object, Mr Pence?"

"I have it, Sir!" Pence drew him over to a nearby table. "Not only have I recovered it, but I have unrolled it. When it's dry, you'll be able to read it – ah! Not yet!" Pence grabbed Devlin's hands. "Don't touch it just yet, Inspector."

Devlin examined the note from a safe distance: it was written in a shaky, backward-slanting hand, with exaggerated loops on certain of the letters. "This was rolled up and shoved in the dead man's ear?" Curiouser and curiouser, Devlin thought, and he didn't even like Lewis Carroll.

"I believe it's a message," Pence said.

"It's unlikely to be his shopping list," Devlin replied. "So there are two notes. Our killer has a penchant for inserting things into the bodily orifices of his victims. That's suggestive, Mr Pence. May I examine a sample of your handwriting?"

"Of course you may, Inspector. I have some recent ledgers here, if you would care to take a look. We keep very careful records: what bodies come in, when they're released and to whom." He brought three notebooks and laid them open on the table in front of Devlin.

Of course. The ledgers were all written in the same hand, an ordinary upright script, without any exaggerated loops and whorls. The two samples could not have been more different. "Thank you, Mr Pence." Devlin glanced over the head again. "So Chimpy died when this note was thrust into his ear?"

Pence blinked. "Of course not, Sir. The eardrum was broken after Mr Darwin was dead. I had a look inside the ear canal; there's almost no bleeding. He died when his throat was cut. If you look here . . ." Pence tilted the head up and back, exposing the neck. "Whoever cut the head off did a hack job, probably with a hand saw or some other serrated instrument. But there's a second cut . . ."

Devlin peered at it through the magnifier; Pence was right. The second cut was slightly higher on the neck and curved upwards, towards the earlobes.

"The second cut is higher on the victim's right side, and also deeper. The carotid arteries on that side were violently cut, almost torn. It's a different blade, too, near as I can tell."

"A left-handed killer," Devlin said. "You'd need something quite sharp to cut a person's throat, isn't that right?"

"Quite sharp, Sir. The cut is very clean. Your average fishmonger wouldn't own a knife like that – couldn't afford a knife like that, even if he knew where to get one."

"So Chimpy was killed by a left-handed man with a love of fine cutlery. Any other injuries?"

"Can't say for certain if there's skull fracture, Sir. I'll know more after I've boiled the head."

Devlin forced back the rising wave of nausea. "Boiled his head?"

"Yes, Sir, with washing soap. The meat drops right off the bone." Pence was a little too gleeful about it.

Devlin caught the lift upstairs and sat down with the first

note. He knew handwriting was easily altered as well as forged: one of the best counterfeiters Devlin ever knew was "Bit-Faker" Beck who'd been taken up for writing bad promissory notes back in the seventies. Beck was completely ambidextrous and could produce some seventeen different hands without even breaking a sweat. Perhaps Whittaker had a stable of friends all waiting on his whims with pens and pencils at the ready.

Dear Boss.

That was taken directly from the Ripper days.

The handwriting was dark and heavy and dappled with many blotches, as though the writer had dipped his pen too far into the inkwell.

You wonder why I send so many presents but I never come to see you.

What presents? Devlin wondered. Perhaps the bodies, left out in the open, and certainly the head. The first full line of writing was as dark as the letter's salutation and scarred with disconnected letters. Some words had been written out in cursive, while others had been printed. The writing slanted backwards, like the note that Pence had found in Chimpy's ear.

Perhaps I'll come and see you soon.

The door of Devlin's office banged back so hard that the knob nearly stuck in the wall. Framed in the entrance was the orange-haired constable with the blizzard of freckles, complete with apologetic expression.

"Beggin' your pardon, Sir, but it's Constable Collins. He says you're to come straightaway."

CHAPTER FIVE

THE BODY WAS lying in the doorway of a chemist's shop, partly screened from traffic by a stack of empty barrels. A young male in his mid-twenties, stylishly dressed, with perhaps an unnecessarily flashy aspect to his tie pin and several jewelled rings upon his fingers. Nothing had been stolen: his watch was still intact, and his billfold still in his pocket, containing a large number of fresh banknotes. The hair had been set on fire, and there was a bloody thumbprint in the middle of his forehead.

"What do you think, Collins?" Devlin bent low over the corpse, his sharp eyes taking in every pertinent detail.

"Oh, I think he's dead, Sir."

Devlin counted to ten before he continued. "You say you

came out of the shop and he was right there, on the doorstep?"

Freddie dutifully flipped open his notebook. "I was inside the shop, talking to the chemist, like you told me."

"And?"

"And I came out and he was there, dead." Freddie licked his fingers and riffled through his notebook. "The man inside says there's a chap comes here every couple weeks or so, buys a lot of different things, not just cologne."

It wouldn't do to presume upon Freddie's investigational skills alone; Devlin posted three burly constables around the body and went inside. The shop was deserted, gloomy and dim; a thin, brittle-looking man was stood on a stepladder stacking parcels near the back. "May I help you?"

"Inspector Devlin, Scotland Yard. I wonder if I could ask you some questions?"

"Of course." The man unfolded himself and came towards them, his arms bent at the elbows and his hands clasped before him in the ages-old attitude of the shopkeeper. "How may I be of assistance?" Even the voice was perfect: dry yet unctuous, and with the practised smugness of a gentleman's butler.

"Constable Collins says you frequently sold bulk quantities of cologne to the same man?"

"Yes."

Devlin blinked. "Would you care to tell me about this man?" Some drifting particles of dust tickled his nose; he turned aside to sneeze. The clerk looked on disdainfully. Perhaps he was disappointed that Devlin didn't wipe his nose in his sleeve.

"I regret, Inspector Dobbin, that I really don't have time."

"Devlin. Make time."

The man's eyebrows rose in a manner befitting Reginald Harker. "Well, er . . . what would you like to know?"

Devlin had memorised the list. "What did he buy, when and how much, does this product contain ambergris, and how often was it purchased? Did he pay with banknotes or did he draft a cheque?" He lit a cigarette and waited.

The man was a young man, the clerk allowed; he came in roughly every two weeks and bought between twenty-four and thirty-six bottles of L'Aventure, a popular scent for gentlemen. L'Aventure contained ambergris as well as other things: vetiver, bergamot and sandalwood. The young man was blond, with a goatee, and rather shabbily dressed, the clerk sniffed.

"If he bought on credit, he would have to sign the ledger, correct?" Another handwriting sample, perhaps, and Devlin would gladly take all the help he could get.

"The gentleman always paid in notes, Sir." Damn.

Freddie hovered near Devlin's shoulder. "Do you habitually record the dates of such purchases?"

Well done, Freddie! "We would like a look at your ledgers," Devlin said. While the clerk disappeared into a back room, Devlin browsed the shelves, taking careful note of their contents. There were huge bottles of hair tonic and preparations for cleaning the teeth; there were chemicals to sweeten the breath (a possible Christmas present for Windigger) and things to chase away the smell of perspiration. There were a great many bottles of scent, including the previously mentioned L'Aventure: Devlin glanced at the price and shuddered. It was well beyond his means. He uncorked it and sniffed: bergamot, some other citrus thing and a bottom note of ambergris. "I will need to retain a bottle of this as evidence," Devlin said. He hefted the bottle in his hand; it was of significant weight.

The clerk's face fell. "L'Aventure is one of our most distinguished scents."

Devlin ignored him and gave the bottle to Freddie. "Now then," he said, bending over the ledgers. Devlin had no head for figures and was for ever thankful that the field of accounting hadn't called to him. "Ah . . . a week and a half ago, twenty-four bottles." He paged back through the ledger, but there was nothing else. "So this mystery gentleman purchased twenty-four bottles of cologne ten days ago?" That put him in the same time frame as the first murder victim. Too bad Harker's chemical findings had been inconclusive: Devlin would have liked a less tenuous link.

"More or less, Inspector." The clerk reached for the ledgers. "If you are finished . . .?"

"Of course."

The clerk snapped the ledger forcefully shut, half an inch from Devlin's nose. "Is there anything else?" he asked. Devlin left his card.

"So he bought some about ten days ago," Freddie said, when they were back outside, "which means, if he's set himself a pattern, he'll be needing to buy more very soon. I daresay it takes more than a sprinkle of the stuff to set someone on fire."

Devlin canted a look at him. "You know, Constable, you really are coming along nicely." He stepped through the phalanx of constables and bent over the body. No blood, no external signs of trauma, and the throat definitely hadn't been cut. Devlin knelt down and pulled the man's cravat away from his neck. "Ah," he said.

"What is it?" Freddie's face loomed large in Devlin's field of vision.

"Finger marks," Devlin said. He pointed them out. "Someone's had their hands around his throat." He reached in and lifted the man's eyelids. "Ah," he said again: the whites of the man's eyes were dappled with tiny red spots. "Broken vessels in the eyes. He's been manually strangled." Devlin was unusually bothered by this: manual strangulation was an intimate way to kill someone. Perhaps the murderer knew his victim and this was a crime of passion, or maybe the killer had altered his usual method, which could mean anything.

"This chap must have really been taking the piss out of him," Freddie remarked. There was a sudden commotion just beyond the door of the shop and angry cries.

Devlin got to his feet. "Constable, secure the scene, if you please. I want no one in or out of here until I say so."

"How dare you lay hands on me? By God, I'll have you on a private prosecution!" The voice fell silent; Reginald Harker stood just inside a circle of constables and stared at the body, his face eerily inscrutable.

"Mr Harker, I'll have to ask you to leave." One of the constables still had hold of Harker's arm and was trying, to no avail, to draw him away.

"Inspector Devlin, this is a mercantile establishment, and I have the right of public thoroughfare!" Harker wrenched himself away.

"It is the scene of a crime, Mr Harker. Please leave."

"How did he . . . what . . . why is Mr Dalziel . . . ? Excuse me." Harker turned and bolted; the sound of vomiting was clearly audible to everyone present.

"What do you suppose that was all about?" Devlin whispered.

"He knows the dead man," Freddie said. "At least, he did." He cast an apologetic look at Devlin. "I've seen them together."

Devlin's scalp prickled. "Where have you seen them together?"

"I'd rather not say."

Devlin nodded. "We will talk about this, Constable." He felt his stomach contract into a cold, hard knot.

"Yes, Sir." Freddie couldn't look at him, but set to examining the corpse.

* * *

Devlin spent the rest of the day poring over the evidence and trying to make some connections. Who was the chemist's strange customer? Apart from the bloody thumbprint, Devlin had no real cause for thinking the murderer was Whittaker; because of the bloody thumbprint, the murderer couldn't be anybody else, because nobody besides Whittaker and Scotland Yard even knew about it. But without any evidence, he hadn't got a case. And what part did Reginald Harker play in all of this? As far as Devlin knew, Harker was (apart from the odd bit of grave robbing) observant of the laws, and had even made a modest name as a pro bono legal advisor to the underclasses. Why, then, would Harker jeopardise himself? It made no sense, yet Freddie knew that Harker and Dalziel had been keeping company, which placed Harker under some degree of suspicion.

After a hurried luncheon at his desk (Freddie was wisely nowhere to be found), Devlin went downstairs to the morgue to see what progress Pence had made on Dalziel's fingernails. But Pence wasn't around and Doyle (his substitute) said Pence had sent a message that he was sick that morning. No, he had nothing about stuff under the fingernails, and couldn't the Inspector see that he had enough on his bloody hands as it was, without worrying about what was under some dead bloke's fingernails? "I wonder if he left a report for me? He said he was going to boil the head."

"Boil the head, did he?" Doyle hawked and spat into one of the drains then wiped his mouth on his sleeve. "He must have taken it home with him, then."

Devlin was rapidly losing patience. "For pity's sake: he must have taken what home with him? The report or the head?"

"Inspector, there's no report and there's no bloody head. As if Nigel would ever write his own reports, the lazy bugger."

"He doesn't . . . he doesn't write?"

"He usually gets me to do it, stands me a jar of gin some-times or maybe a pint. Says he's allergic to the paper we use round here, although he can write well enough at other times." Doyle sucked some mucus into the back of his throat. "Lazy sod."

"So any records kept down here, any entries in the ledgers, signatures for the release of bodies are made by you." This case was thicker than Thames sludge, Devlin thought.

"Right. If I left it for Nigel, it'd never get done. That's the way it is, Guv'nor. And I'm glad enough to do it, as long as he keeps me in pints and the like." Doyle hitched up his trousers. "Now if you'll excuse me, I've got work to do."

Devlin thought about going after him and decided against it. Doyle was enormous, more than six feet tall and quite burly. Besides, there was nothing to be gained by harassing an employee.

He went back upstairs and made himself a cup of tea; without Freddie's expert touch it tasted stale and flat, and he ended up tossing it down the drain. He wandered into the archives room and forgot what he was looking for, so he went down to the sergeants' room and lifted the newspaper. It was the usual thing: overturned carts in Covent Garden, stolen handkerchiefs in Whitehall, omnibus accident in Charing Cross. Nothing today about the most recent murder, which meant one of two things: either Abernathy didn't know about it, or he did know and Neville Alcock had taken steps to shut him up. Abernathy hadn't come near the shop where Dennis Dalziel had been found, but news travelled at lightning speed around the Yard, and an open case was hardly a secret. Maybe – here Devlin allowed himself a smile – maybe Sir Neville had warned Abernathy off. It was an immensely cheering thought.

Freddie had seen Harker with Dennis Dalziel on at least one occasion. Freddie had recognised Dalziel lying in the shop doorway.

He's one of them as well. Of course it wasn't immediately apparent: why would it be? If Freddie recognised Dalziel on sight, he'd definitely seen him more than once. How could Devlin have missed it? How could he not have known Freddie's inclinations? But Devlin didn't really know Freddie at all. Mrs Alcock's tea dance was the only time he and Freddie had socialised, apart from last year's Christmas party – which had been a fracas in every sense of the word. Devlin had spent the evening in a corner with Abernathy, both of them drunk and surly, trading insults above the din, while Freddie made the rounds and charmed everyone within reach.

Devlin experienced a sudden, uncharacteristic urge to rush to Freddie and tell him everything, confess, make a clean breast of it. (He'd never understood that saying.) The clergy were fond of it, weren't they? Always on at people to confess, get things off their chest, clear the air, so why not tell Freddie the whole truth, instead of the edited version he'd given Alcock? Alcock was aware that Devlin was acquainted with Whittaker and that they had been at school together, but that was only half the story. Yes, why not tell Freddie, and then strangle him so he could never tell Alcock, which he'd have to do as soon as it came out Devlin's mouth. He couldn't imagine being called into Alcock's office and asked about it: *What do you have to say about this, Devlin?*

He couldn't imagine telling the truth: that Whittaker had coerced and tortured him, bullied him relentlessly for years until he was almost out of his mind with it. Without money or influence or a powerful father, Devlin was nothing at that school: a working-class misfit seriously out of his depth amongst the upper classes. Devlin's father was a police detective – certainly not a member of the Peerage, or anything like it – and, while his mother did have servants, they hardly lived in the kind of palatial luxury that Whittaker had been used to. A family legacy paid for Devlin's schooling, for his books and clothing, but beyond that, there was nothing extra. And Whittaker had been bounced out of every other decent school in Britain, and so found himself on the end of a precipitously short tether. It was all Whittaker at that school, and everybody knew it. Whittaker travelled with a hand-picked group of minions, all of whom were loyal to him, ready to do his bidding. He and his friends had made Devlin do things, had kept him in thrall to them, in the age-old manner of schoolboys. Because of it (and other things, but best not to go into those just now), Devlin expected horrible things to happen to him, even now, and was for ever waiting for the next disaster. Perhaps this was why he'd chosen the Force, because it at least gave him the option of meeting the horrid things head-on.

He shook off the reverie; he'd been staring at the same page for the last five minutes, while the past raked its claws over him. He tossed the newspaper in the rubbish bin and resolved to spend the afternoon in productive study of the evidence. It was nearly five when Devlin glanced up to see Freddie Collins step into the office, already in his overcoat and carrying his gloves. "If you're not needing me any more tonight, Sir, I thought I'd dodge along."

"So Dennis Dalziel and Harker had been keeping company." Devlin pushed aside the papers he'd been examining and turned his full attention on Freddie.

"Sir."

"You saw them together."

"I didn't think . . . where I saw them . . ." He wouldn't meet Devlin's gaze, but kept his eyes fixed on the floor.

"Where did you see them? In the street? At Mr Harker's?"

Freddie whispered something Devlin couldn't quite make out.

"Beg your pardon?"

"A molly house, Sir. I . . . I was in a molly house."

"A molly house." Devlin's hands were shaking; he clasped them together under the desk. It couldn't be the truth. It wasn't possible. Granted, he'd never seen Freddie with a woman, but such an observation counted for nothing. A young constable, without the means to marry and perhaps without any prospects . . . for all he knew Freddie had a sweetheart in every parlour in London.

"It's a place where men go, Sir . . . when they want the company of other men." Freddie's face was bright red, and beads of sweat dotted his high forehead. He swiped at his eyes awkwardly, too ashamed of his tears to let them fall.

"I know what it is, Constable." Devlin allowed himself to breathe. So this was Freddie's awful secret, a predilection for the company of his own sex?

"I'll hand in my warrant card, shall I, Sir?" Freddie laid it and his darbies on the desk.

"What the devil for?" Devlin pushed them away. "No

crime has been committed. Unless you've been discovered in flagrante with a renter . . . ?"

"No, Sir. No renters." Freddie managed a shaky smile.

"Then, since no crime has been committed, I can hardly accept your resignation. Take back your warrant card, Constable, and put those bracelets somewhere safe." Devlin pretended not to notice as Freddie scrubbed his sleeve across his eyes. "That'll be all."

"Thank you, Sir."

"Good night." He turned back to the growing pile of evidence at his elbow, feigning interest in the handwritten notes and listening to Freddie's footsteps drifting down the stairs. Devlin was halfway through a second reading of the hatbox note when he suddenly sat bolt upright and yelled loud enough to be heard in the cleaner's closet in the basement. Three largish sewer rats and a prostitute by the name of Boompin' Nelly appropriately scattered, thinking that the ungodly scream had been uttered at the instant of the Final Judgement.

Devlin caught up with Freddie on the pavement just outside the door and seized on him with both hands. "This club," he panted. "Are you going there tonight? Are you going to the molly house?"

Two aged sisters returning from an afternoon's perusal of the merchantware in Covent Garden wheeled an extreme berth around Devlin and drew their shawls protectively around them. "Keep your voice down!" Freddie hissed. "Are you telling everyone that I'm . . ."

Devlin clapped a hand over the taller man's mouth. "Are you

going to the club tonight?" He spoke with the exaggerated slowness usually directed at lunatics and the hard of hearing.

Freddie, his speech constrained by Devlin's hand, nodded vigorously.

"Any one of them could be a target. He's already done Dennis Dalziel; God only knows who might be next." Devlin was musing aloud now, his quick mind skipping rapidly over possibilities, alternately choosing and rejecting strategies as quickly as his brain disgorged them. "I want to go there and have a look around, question some of the, er . . . patrons. Someone might have seen something, heard Whittaker talking. Maybe he's luring victims like the Ripper did."

Freddie disengaged Devlin's hand from his lips. "Think he's pretending to be a toff?"

Devlin levelled a glance at the young constable. "John Whittaker doesn't have to play at being a toff. He's one of them, and every bit as degenerate as they are."

* * *

Devlin was as uncomfortable as ever in his life, even though the circumstances of his current situation contained no overt goads to his morality, no pricks to his conscience. Devlin found himself frowning, thinking that perhaps "prick" was an unfortunate choice of word, considering the venue.

For half an hour he'd sat beside Constable Collins at a lavishly appointed banquette; for twenty-nine and a half minutes Constable Collins had had his hand on Devlin's thigh. It was, Devlin thought, playing it a bit too close to the bone.

The entertainment consisted of a rather vapid floor show, wherein young men dressed in frocks mounted – here Devlin chided himself severely for the paucity of his personal lexicon – a low stage and crooned the collected works of Mr Gilbert and Mr Sullivan. The real entertainment, Devlin thought, was in the club itself, which presented the same overall sentiment as a knacker's yard the day after a particularly bad showing at Ascot.

He saw men openly engage each other for assignations, all within his earshot, and couples ascending the stairs into some shadowy region high above, their arms around each other, their faces close together. Devlin wondered what on earth could possibly be upstairs, but he was willing to bet it had something to do with lust and secrets, things better undertaken in the dark.

A tall form loomed over Devlin, and a smiling blond figure leaned down and caressed his cheek with one elegantly manicured finger. "Hit me," the figure whispered.

Devlin's collar was suddenly too tight and he felt confused. "I beg your pardon?"

The figure offered Devlin the handle of a whip: a quirt or riding crop, a strip of stinging leather. Devlin was suddenly and unpleasantly reminded of the headmaster of his schooldays, who liked to put boys over his bended knees and administer a caning. Perhaps, Devlin mused, his old headmaster was here.

"Oh, come on . . . give us a few whacks, Guv'nor."

Devlin felt faint. He pushed out from underneath Collins's clutching hand. "Lavatory," he whispered.

This seemed to inflame the whip-bearing gorgon to entirely new heights. "Like it in the lavvies, do ya, Guv'nor?"

Devlin plunged through the crowd of men with a kind of maniacal desperation. He felt as though he were trapped in a particularly devious nightmare, and all he could see in front of him were the backs of men and the faces of men, smiling mouths leering wetly under waxed moustaches. He gained the relative safety of the lavatory and leaned against the door, trying to calm his racing heart. Behind his closed eyelids he could see the lurid glances of the stage performers, whinnying their songs to a somewhat less than rapt audience. It was all too sordid.

"Inspector Devlin!" The familiar summons gripped him with a flare of panic; he opened his eyes cautiously, uncertain of what he might find.

Harker had never looked better: the dark suit he wore set off his strange green eyes with a particular inevitability, as if some malicious destiny had decreed that he meet Devlin here in the toilets.

"Mr Harker."

"Ah, Devlin . . ." Harker smiled gently. "I am sorry that your post mortem efforts on behalf of your charred bodies did not yield more promising results. Donnelly and I both tried our best."

"Terrible about Mr Dalziel," Devlin murmured. "Did you know him well?" What the devil was Harker doing here, Devlin wondered, and more to the point, did his naturally inquisitive mind lead him to make suppositions about Devlin that would prove to be of a devastating truth?

"He and I were sometime partners at cards."

"Cards." Perhaps it was a euphemism?

"Only cards, Inspector." Harker was leaning on the door in what could only be construed as a proprietary manner. His gaze flickered on Devlin's face, travelled to Devlin's throat, his practised eye entirely appreciative of Devlin's appearance.

"Cards." Devlin couldn't seem to make his vocal cords work; he was mesmerised by the glint in Harker's eyes. Harker knew his secrets; Harker understood him in a way that no one else could.

"You have always made much of the distances between us, Devlin . . ." Harker was standing too close to him. "And yet, I see that we are truly not so different."

Devlin's pulse was pounding in his ears. *He knows.* He should turn round immediately and go out the door, turn in his handcuffs and his warrant card, get out of the country before it all came out and ruined him.

"Rest easy, Inspector." Harker straightened his tie with the aplomb that Devlin had always envied and never been able to achieve. "You have nothing to fear from me. Indeed, your secret is quite safe."

"I don't know what you're talking about," Devlin said. His mind was filled with a huge, forbidding image: the great treadmill at Pentonville, five hours a day every day, for years and years until his punishment was served or he died from the strain of it.

Devlin straightened his necktie and pushed the lavatory doors open. Harker had already gone. His knees were shaking as he made his way back to Freddie.

"Are you all right?" Freddie asked.

"Fine," Devlin croaked.

"You don't look fine," the constable said. "Has anybody been bothering you?" He adopted an expression of knowing insouciance that was just this side of a smirk. "The lads get a bit rowdy when a handsome new man comes to visit."

Devlin was just about to reprimand Freddie for his cheek when a flurry of movement caught his attention. "That's Nigel Pence," he declared.

"From the morgue?" Freddie craned his neck. "Where?"

"Stay here." Devlin pushed himself away from the table, his pulse thumping angrily in his ears. Off sick, was he? At home boiling a head, was he? He caught Pence by the shoulder and spun him round. "Mr Pence."

Pence glanced at him – the fleering, lip-curled glance of a hunted animal – and bolted, disappearing into the crowd. Devlin gave chase, leaping neatly over a chair, a pair of boots and a rather savage-looking dwarf who snarled and raised his fist. Devlin pursued as quickly as he could, but Pence was still ahead of him, slipping easily through the thronging crowd of men and occasionally glancing round to see if Devlin was following. Devlin caught up with him in front of the bar, grabbed his shoulder. "I just want to talk to you, man!" Pence twisted away from him and ran, darting under the outstretched arms of what was possibly the tallest woman Devlin had ever seen. The woman had an enormous powdered bosom and a handlebar moustache, and a tattoo on the side of her neck: DYE TRYING.

"Nigel, wait!" Pence tripped; Devlin winced as the young

man went sprawling on the floor. As he reached out to help Pence up, someone slammed into him and sent him flying into a stand of potted aspidistra. He regained his feet, only to be shoved off balance by a trio of giddy revellers who jollied him round and round in circles, laughing like fishwives on Good Friday.

"Take my hand, Sir." Freddie's voice reached him somehow through the din. "Oi! Shove off, you lot!" The constable pulled him upright and dusted him down. "All right, Sir?"

"Where is he?" Devlin scanned the crowd.

Pence had vanished. Devlin swore, a satisfying stream of curses that fortunately went unheard: the floorshow had resumed, and the gentlemen in frocks had changed their repertoire from Gilbert and Sullivan to a bastardised can-can.

"Afraid he's gone, Sir." Freddie touched his elbow. "Should we go after him?"

"No," Devlin said. "I'll find him at the Yard."

He gathered his dignity and left.

*　*　*

Devlin always prided himself on being at least outwardly circumspect, on keeping his "proclivities" strictly to himself. Even after all these years, it would be hard to pick a man out of the general community who would point at him and immediately declare him deviant. He had become singularly adept at hiding his true nature, even to the point of not revealing his real name to those men with whom he had pursued relations. He knew what Harker was and he knew what Donnelly was, knew that the absurd euphemisms employed by society stood for very little. Donnelly at least had common sense enough to be discreet, but Harker's eccentricities, Devlin knew, would be his own undoing. Strictly speaking, Devlin could have arrested both of them under the aegis of the Act and pursued it as he would any other criminal matter. As it stood he was putting the entire Metropolitan Police Force in jeopardy of ridicule by turning a wilfully blind eye to what went on at 12½ Fowler Street. It was a strange sort of dance that he was doing, Devlin mused, wondering whom to trust and when to keep his mouth shut. And Harker knew the bent of Devlin's proclivities (he'd made that abundantly clear), and perhaps someday Harker might tell. But Devlin knew what Harker was, and he doubted the solicitor welcomed a prospective stay at Reading Gaol or Newgate.

He got up from his desk, went to look at himself in the mirror: a slender man of early middle age, with a thin face, eyes probably larger and more naive than was strictly necessary for a man of his profession. Those of the Yard whom he counted among his friends (they were precious few) were inclined to overlook his rather hungry-looking eagerness.

"Sir?" Freddie Collins appeared in the doorway. "Any news?"

"News about what?" Devlin asked, rather more sharply than intended. "News about the murderer, or whether anyone else has turned up with a bloody thumbprint somewhere on his body? News about Nigel Pence and why the devil he isn't at work today?" Devlin crossed to his desk and gazed pointedly into his empty mug. "Cup of tea wouldn't go amiss."

Freddie was unfazed. "Right you are, Guv. Oh, by the bye, there's a couple of ladies here to see you."

Devlin experienced a flash of panic. Perhaps someone had discovered him and had come to lodge a complaint of public lewdness. Some hairy-chinned bluestocking, no doubt outraged by such a defamation of the Yard's inherent moral character, had decided to make an example of him. It would be all over the newspapers, a public scandal or worse.

"Who are they, Constable?" He fought to make his voice sound normal.

"One of 'em is all got up in gentleman's togs and smoking a cigar." Evidently Freddie found nothing odd in this. "And the other one is Miss Phoebe Alcock."

"Phoebe Alcock?" Devlin checked his watch. "At this hour?"

She appeared in a cloud of costly perfume, decked out in what seemed to Devlin to be some sort of split skirt: a bicycling costume. Slightly behind her there came a tall young redhead dressed like Lord Byron. "Mrs Violet Pearson," Phoebe introduced her to Devlin and Freddie. "My most intimate friend." Mrs Pearson stepped forward as if submitting herself to a duel and shook Devlin's hand with a certain manly vigour. Just as quickly as Devlin had made this paragon's acquaintance, Phoebe was dismissing her: "Run along now, Violet, and play with Constable Collins. I need to chat with this gorgeous boy alone."

Freddie grudgingly offered Mrs Pearson his arm, clearly resentful of being left out of the proceedings. "I'll give you a tour," Freddie said, and darted a sharp look at Devlin.

"Only approved areas, Constable. Stay out of the morgue," Devlin said, in case Freddie's current level of pique might seduce him into showing their visitor rather more than was acceptable.

"Can I see your darbies?" Violet Pearson's voice floated up the stairwell as they disappeared. Devlin waited until he was absolutely sure they had gone.

"Your *intimate* friend?"

Phoebe reached over and took a cigarette from the box on Devlin's desk. "The Queen herself has declared that such acts do not occur between women."

Devlin permitted himself a short, cynical laugh. "I knew a woman once in Stepney Green who made herself a fortune catering to both."

Phoebe took his chin between her finger and thumb. "Still not sleeping, I see." Before Devlin could make a suitable rejoinder, she said, "Elizabeth Hobbs."

"Where did you hear that name?" He spoke as quickly as he could, to prevent his bottom lip from quivering *Be objective*, he told himself, *it was just another case*. He reached into his pocket for his handkerchief, mopped his sweating forehead.

"It was something Father let drop one night, at the supper table."

Devlin stared at her, incredulous. "He let it drop? At supper?" The only thing Devlin could imagine Old Brassie dropping at supper was his fork, and that tragedy alone would be enough to precipitate an international incident.

"It's not the point, Inspector. I know all about Dennis

Dalziel. I know what he was. I know that he was killed and set on fire in a doorway. I know he was a pouf, Inspector. One only had to look at him to see it."

Devlin was thinking about the way the hair on Dalziel's head had burned, and the bloody thumbprint. "I don't know where you got that information, Miss Alcock, but might I remind you that you are discussing official police business."

"I know why you never married." Her gaze was clear, steady and without compromise. The clock on the wall ticked relentlessly behind her, as measured and steady as a metronome. Devlin saw the end of everything: he'd be condemned as a sodomite, subject to the harshest of penalties, because he was a copper, and corrupt, in open defiance of the Act. Devlin turned a horrified gaze on Phoebe Alcock, a gaze full of fear and patent misery.

"I have a proposition for you." She touched his arm, broke into a smile. "Oh, for God's sake, Inspector, don't look at me like that!"

Blackmail, Devlin thought, *she's going to blackmail me.* What resources had he, on a policeman's salary?

"I think this is something you will readily agree to, Inspector." She took his hands in hers and squeezed them gently. "If we can agree on terms, I think everything will work out to your benefit." She sank into a chair and removed her gloves slowly, a finger at a time. It was a studied gesture, the gesture of a courtesan; Devlin wondered where she'd learned it and why she was using it now. "I find myself in an awkward situation, Inspector, as far as my parents are concerned."

Devlin's heart thumped noisily in his chest. "Miss Alcock, I really haven't the time for games. If you have a point to make, do make it."

"I should like to be seen with you," she said.

"Seen with me?"

"About London, at parties, riding on a Sunday afternoon in Rotten Row, that sort of thing."

Devlin remembered the last time he'd been on a horse; it had ended badly. He'd been seven, and the horse was a Shetland pony. What the devil was Phoebe playing at?

"I'm not sure why you would want to engage in such a pointless charade. Unless I did something at your dear mamma's tea dance that I don't remember?"

Phoebe smiled. "Violet and I love each other. My father has started making marriage noises, saying how I ought to find myself an eligible young man and settle down." She leaned forward. "Understand, Inspector, that I have absolutely no intention of leaving Violet. When time and circumstances permit, we intend to set up permanent housekeeping together. Right now I'm lodging with Violet at her house in Kensington, but we have made plans to go abroad.

"Violet's husband Edgar was in India you know, an army officer. He came from a very good family, and when he died his wealth passed to Violet. It was an unfortunate hunting accident, but then tigers are quite unpredictable." Phoebe smiled.

"And what makes you think I won't run to your father and tell him everything that you've just told me?"

"That would be a regrettable choice, Inspector. I'm afraid

I would have to expose you. I wonder what Father would say if he knew one of his inspectors was a raving pouf?"

Devlin held himself expressionless. "If I even knew what you were on about, Miss Alcock, I might be able to frame a suitable reply. Is there anything else? Only I'm terribly busy."

She rose to go. "Do this for me, Inspector, and I will hold your secret safe till the grave."

"And if I don't?"

She reached into her reticule and handed him an envelope; Devlin recognised his own handwriting immediately. He recognised, too, the circumstances which had prompted the letter, and he remembered all too well his correspondent.

"John Whittaker," Phoebe said.

Devlin's throat constricted. "That was years ago."

"The Metropolitan Police Force would hardly care if it were years ago or yesterday, Inspector." She slipped her gloves on. "Don't bother looking inside for the letter, I have it in a safe place with all the others."

Devlin got up, moved around the desk. "Give me my letters."

"I'm afraid I can't do that." She regarded him with what might be sympathy under other circumstances. "Perhaps we'll start with a nice afternoon walk? Some day soon. I'll come round and fetch you."

Devlin escorted her down to the main door, terrified that she might make a detour into her father's office and tell the old man everything. His mind was churning with the import of what had just passed between them: mainly he wondered if she would make good on her promises.

"Let us just keep the entire matter quiet for now, Inspector." She smiled, stood on tiptoe and kissed him. "And here's Violet! Did you enjoy your tour, my dear?"

In the subsequent babble of female conversation, and before he fled headlong back up to his office, Devlin caught a glimpse of Freddie Collins.

The constable looked as if Devlin had slapped him.

CHAPTER SIX

ALONE IN THE archives room, Freddie Collins carefully reconsidered what he'd just seen pass between Phoebe Alcock and Devlin. Of course, anyone would want to kiss Devlin, he reasoned, and even if Devlin was shockingly unaware of his own appeal, that made him no less attractive to others. What in God's name had Devlin been doing? The simplest explanation was that Devlin liked his bread buttered on either side or both. He suspected, although he couldn't know for certain, that Devlin had at some time engaged in one or two brief affairs with men, of mild interest and short duration, but he'd never seen Devlin with a woman, except Phoebe Alcock. And yet Devlin had spent much of his free time at the tea dance in the garden, drinking with Phoebe Alcock and doing God knew what.

Beyond the table where he was working, something dropped. Freddie froze in place, his senses turned toward the direction of the sound. "Bugger," he murmured. "Losing me bloody mind, I am." Then he heard it again: a discrete click, like roundshot being dispensed into a tin. The tiny hairs on the back of his neck rose, and he wondered if it would be cowardly for a constable of the Metropolitan Police to run screaming out the door. "Get a hold of yourself," he said. "Nobody in here but you." He glanced around and then concentrated on the work at hand.

Freddie knew the Whittaker file, and there was no real reason why he should need to consult it, except he couldn't face Devlin at the moment and thought it better to stay out of the inspector's way. The file was all of a piece, a detailed record of Whittaker's previous rampage through the city: a series of bloody assaults on the same police officer (Devlin); causing a disturbance in a public place (the rat pit at the Blue Anchor sporting club); physical assault on a female minor (thirteen-year-old Fanny LaMont, daughter of a Spitalfields weaver); and finally, the murder of Elizabeth Hobbs. Devlin's initial report said that Whittaker had held her out of the window of an empty house in Camden House Road; he'd set her on fire by igniting the wig she wore and pushed her out the window. A bloody thumbprint had been laid on her thigh and somehow survived. The police surgeon at the time had been one Norris Pence; he'd released the body into the care of the Poor Relief. Freddie noted that Devlin had initiated a burial fund to pay for Hobbs's tombstone.

A slight movement by a far bank of files caught Freddie's attention; his immediate field of vision blurred, interrupted by a wide swath of black, and a man in a black topcoat was peering down at him and smiling. There was something the matter with his face: the two sides didn't match, like they'd been badly glued together. Freddie's pulse thudded in his ears.

"Who the devil are you?"

"Does Phillip remember?" The man leaned close, gazing at the young constable with real interest. "Does he understand at all what this means?" He reached out and laid one gloved finger on Freddie's mouth. "Shh. Don't answer. There's time for that. There will be time for everything, eventually."

Freddie stood up so fast his chair shot out from under him and crashed into the opposite wall. "Fuck off out of it," he snarled, "or else." But he was talking to himself; there was no longer anyone in the archives room but him.

* * *

"Where's Constable Collins?" Devlin stopped at the desk on his way out, pulling on his gloves with half his mind elsewhere.

"I haven't seen him, Guv." The sergeant applied himself studiously to the procedures manual lying open in front of him, affecting an expression of great intelligence that sadly failed to convince even himself.

"How long have you been on duty here?"

What the hell was Phoebe Alcock thinking? Devlin had passed from shock and fear to a state of patent anger.

"Half an hour, Sir."

Devlin nodded. "I have pressing business to attend to. If you see him, tell him I'll be back later on." Devlin buttoned up his overcoat against the October chill. "And by the way, Sergeant . . ."

"Sir?"

"Your bloody book is upside down!"

* * *

John Donnelly kept an office of sorts in Kensington, but where exactly in Kensington, Devlin was not entirely sure, and so spent nearly an hour clopping about in a hansom cab with a not entirely helpful cabbie suggesting possible venues. Had Donnelly been a proper chemist, he would have perhaps taken the ground floor of a house and made it into a shop, but Donnelly wasn't now and never had been a proper chemist, merely a bounder from an Essex family just recently risen into the middle classes. Donnelly made great pretence about being forced out of school before he'd completed his training, but Devlin had done some checking and knew that Donnelly's downfall had been a badly restrained hunger for sexual congress in public places. He'd been caught fondling a fellow student on the boat train during summer holidays, in the years before the amendment to the Act, and so had avoided imprisonment. His return to school, however, saw him on the wrong end of a private prosecution and summarily expelled. He'd managed to gather enough skills to set himself up as a sort of backroom chemist, but Devlin knew that Donnelly's sometimes lavish lifestyle and taste for gambling were largely funded by Reginald Harker.

The Donnelly premises were located in a respectable looking house with an unassuming brick front and a brass plaque beside the door proclaiming that here was one Mr John Hector Donnelly, apothecary and chemist. The door opened on to a pleasant anteroom, comfortably furnished and boasting several large potted ferns. There was no one in the reception area; Devlin hallooed the corridor, with no reply. He chose a chair nearest the window and browsed through a months-old copy of *The Strand* that he'd found lying behind a flowerpot. After some moments, a door opened, and Donnelly appeared, clad in a long white apron that was decorated with sundry bits of gore. "Inspector! What a surprise. Please, do come in!"

"I hope I'm not catching you at a bad time?" Devlin wasn't sure where the blood and guts had come from, and he wasn't about to ask: it was not altogether impossible that Donnelly had been engaged in some dissection work for Harker, for reasons better left to the imagination.

"Not at all, not at all." Donnelly ushered Devlin into his consulting room and went immediately to wash his hands at the basin, taking great care to scrub his fingers and his nails. The filthy apron, however, he chose to retain. "Now then, my dear fellow, what can I do for you?"

Devlin decided to dispense with preamble. "How long can a person be infected with syphilis before the, ah, final stages?"

Donnelly regarded Devlin with narrowed eyes. "That depends," he replied. "You might want to get undressed."

"What for?" he asked, trying hard to keep a note of truculence out of his voice.

"Well, I'd very much like to examine you, to see how far the infection has already progressed. Just slip out of your clothes and get under the blanket."

"Not me!" Devlin's head had begun to pound. "I ask merely out of professional interest."

Donnelly seemed relieved. "Well, of course, and I mean, you couldn't have caught it just from that one night at the Peacock Club."

"I see you've been talking to Harker."

"We occupy the same rooms, Inspector." Donnelly smiled coyly. "Pillow talk, you know. Post-coitus, the powers of conversation are rather heightened."

"All right, all right," Devlin conceded the point irritably. "But how long does it take?"

"After the secondary symptoms," Donnelly launched into his task with real enthusiasm, "that is, after the, er, genital nodule disappears . . . well, the disease sometimes goes into a long latency period, without any ill effects. There would be no external evidence that the person had been infected and no indication of illness."

Devlin sagged visibly. "Damn," he whispered.

Donnelly appeared not to have heard him. "Latency, in some cases, can last a lifetime, unless other organs are involved. Of course, the worst is neurosyphilis, when, in the tertiary stages, the brain is involved. There are documented case histories of patients in lunatic asylums –"

"Thank you, Mr Donnelly. That will do nicely. Very help-ful." He cast a parting glance at Donnelly's soiled apron. "When you see Mr Harker, would you ask him to call on me, at the Yard? There are some aspects of the case I am very eager to discuss with him." Probably not those features which Harker expected, but nevertheless . . .

"I haven't seen him very much lately. He does pursue an after-hours existence these days. Of course he's always had an artistic bent. His grandmother was French, you know."

Doubtless Harker was even then settled comfortably in a café somewhere, discussing Truth, Beauty and Life with an audience of enraptured young catamites at his feet. Devlin turned to go.

"One more thing, Inspector."

"Yes?"

"The patient – this poor wretch with tertiary syphilis – who is he?"

Devlin hesitated. "He's . . . no one, Mr Donnelly. A speculation."

CHAPTER SEVEN

DEVLIN SPENT THE next several days in a state of inertia, dealing with run-of-the-mill cases and fending off enquiries from Abernathy about Whittaker and the murders and the head. The weather turned bitterly cold, with a relentless wind blowing from the north, chilling all and sundry and flaying the edges of already frayed nerves. Devlin dreaded the walk each morning, and took to leaving his rooms with three or four heavy woolen scarves round his head and two pairs of gloves. He invariably arrived at his desk with a red nose and streaming eyes, shivering violently and wanting nothing more than to crawl inside the teapot and stay there until summer.

"Has he brought the head back?" Abernathy cornered

Devlin in the lift one morning. "You've not seen him, have you? He's run off with that head, and it's all your fault."

"Why the devil would Pence run off with a human head?" Devlin snapped. "Best keep your nose out of it, George. It's my case, now." He waited till Abernathy had gone, then sprinted down the stairs to the morgue; Pence was not there. Devlin questioned the police surgeon, an extremely old man who was retained on half-pay because it kept him out of the gin palace.

"Who?" The surgeon was quite deaf and nearly blind; he peered at Devlin owlishly and blinked several times in rapid succession, like Adam newly awakened to consciousness by God. "Who?"

"Nigel Pence," Devlin explained; "he works here. Have you seen him?"

But his enquiries proved fruitless. Before the old doctor could launch into a long recollection of his days as a field surgeon during the Crimean War, complete with bursting shells and rifle pops, Devlin left him to it and dispatched two junior constables to Pence's address in hopes of finding him at home. They reported back that his lodgings were deserted and Pence himself was nowhere to be seen.

Devlin found Freddie in his office, bent over a broken teapot. A great amount of fine Ceylon leaf had puddled on the top of Devlin's desk, and Freddie was trying to mop it up with his one sorry handkerchief. "Sorry, Sir. Teapot got away from me."

"Leave it," Devlin said. "You know, Constable, we've made piss-all progress on this case thus far. For all we know,

Whittaker could be out there right now, carving some poor bugger's insides out." There had been no further communication from the murderer, no notes, no body parts, nothing. It was as if Whittaker had vanished into thin air.

"Maybe he's died, Sir." Freddie dropped the broken pieces of teapot in the bin.

"Oh, of course," Devlin said. "Repented of his evil ways and thrown himself in front of the Metropolitan Line? Jumped into the Thames? I doubt it." The lack of knowledge gnawed at him: as long as Whittaker remained hidden, Devlin was as blind as a mole, and the case could progress no further. He needed Whittaker out in the open, where he could get at him.

"Sir." Freddie was hovering.

"Yes, Constable?"

"Well, I was thinking, Sir."

God help us, Devlin remarked silently. "And?"

"If the murderer was buying lots of cologne from that shop, then he'd need some way to carry it all home, wouldn't he? Especially in the quantities he was buying."

Devlin nodded. What was Freddie driving at, and was it something that Devlin himself had overlooked? "Those bottles were made of significant glass. All fancy cut, quite heavy and quite expensive."

"Well, Sir, if he's buying a lot of this stuff, he can't be carrying it very far, not unless he's got his own gang of navvies. He must live near by." Freddie stopped abruptly, suddenly bereft of thoughts.

"How much does a bottle of cologne weigh, Constable?"

Devlin began rummaging through drawers. "A few ounces, perhaps?" He unearthed the bottle of L'Aventure he had taken from the shop. "You've got the liquid, which weighs nearly nothing . . ."

"Mostly alcohol and water," Freddie said.

". . . and then you've got the bottle." Devlin tossed it to Freddie, who caught it neatly.

"Cor, this thing weighs a ton," Freddie said.

"So the clerk said he was buying a case of this at a time. It doesn't make sense, though . . . if he's buying it to start fires, why not buy something cheaper? Why not start the fire with gin, for goodness' sake?"

Freddie considered. "He's telling us something, isn't he? He's telling us he's rich enough to buy it and throw it about like that."

"But if he's rich, why isn't he living in Kensington? Why hasn't he got a mansion in Hampstead?"

"Not many renters in Hampstead, Sir."

Devlin leapt up as though he'd been set on fire. "Into your coat, Constable."

* * *

For over an hour they scoured the area around the chemist's shop. Devlin assiduously avoided going inside, in case the clerk might ask for his bottle back. "Any rooms to let in the area, I wonder?"

"They wouldn't be to let now, Sir. If he's living here, they'd be let already."

"Right." They began a systematic search of the properties

surrounding the area, but Devlin didn't really expect to find anything: it was like looking for one small thing in an enormous pile of other small things.

"Needle in a haystack, Sir?"

Obviously he'd spoken aloud without realising it. "Something like that, Constable." They were in front of an imposing three-storey building with a battery of locks on the windows and door; Devlin seized the knocker and rapped it sharply.

"Are we just going to walk in, Sir? Maybe the landlady won't want any coppers nosing round."

"Watch and learn, Constable."

A large, round woman appeared in the doorway, brandishing a broom in one hand and a bucket in the other: two tiny brown eyes resided in the squashed folds of fat, and her enormous breasts appeared capable of higher motor function. She smelled of tripe and onions and old sweat. "I don't give to no charity cases," she said.

She made to shut the door but Devlin stuck his foot in it. "He's got my umbrella."

"Who?" Her small eyes narrowed even further. "Who the devil are you talking about?"

"Your lodger: tall man, wears a black top hat and gloves. Got my umbrella and I'm to get it back from him. It's a family heirloom, the last thing my poor old father gave me." It was a gamble, but perhaps for once the odds would fall in his favour.

"He's probably run off with it, then. That bugger owes me rent, and all." She regarded them both, her gaze lingering especially long on Freddie. "Right. You might as well go up, then. Only don't touch anything and don't take anything besides your umbrella."

She herded them up the stairs, her stentorian breathing a harsh counterpoint to Devlin's pounding heart. If his hunches were correct, this was Whittaker's current place of residence; in an ideal world, Whittaker would be waiting for them, expecting them, and he would go quietly when Devlin snapped the cuffs on him.

Not bloody likely.

"He's a quiet sort," the landlady said, "likes to keep to himself. Lovely manners, but there's something wrong with his face." She peered at Devlin intently, her small eyes examining him, judging him. "It's all burned, like, on one side. That your friend? And what's he living here for, a toff like him?" She raised her fist and Devlin jumped back; she hammered on the door several times in rapid succession and waited. There was no sound except their commingled breaths and the noise of the wind outside; clearly their quarry had gone out. Devlin shot a look at Freddie and pushed past the landlady and into the flat.

The windows were shrouded in heavy drapes, and the lack of light cast a pall of gloom over everything. Devlin could make out a fireplace mantel and the settee opposite, and a dining table somewhere towards the back of the room. A fine layer of dust had spread over everything in sight, and a plate of half-eaten food lay mouldering on the floor by the settee; the mantel clock had stopped. Someone had stacked recent editions of all the newspapers near the fireplace;

Devlin could just make out the headlines. A pair of sleeve links glimmered from the mantelpiece; Devlin leaned close to examine them. "They're his," he said.

"Whittaker's sleeve links?" Freddie reached for them.

Devlin held the young man's hand away. "The entwined J and W, you see? These were a gift from his father. He wore them at school; I remember them. There's a scratch on the back of one. He dropped it between some paving stones in Kentish Town while we were on a school trip." Devlin dropped them into an envelope. "I should have told you that Whittaker and I were at school together." It wasn't quite an apology. "That day at Fowler Street."

"Maybe someone stole them," Freddie pointed out. "And put them here for us to find."

"It's possible," Devlin allowed, "but why go to all the trouble? Why steal something as insignificant as a set of sleeve links when you could steal a man's watch or the contents of his wallet? If you're going to have a lamb chop, Constable, you might as well have the whole sheep."

Freddie frowned. "I don't even like mutton."

Three doors were set into the adjacent wall; Devlin pushed open the first one gingerly. "Lavatory," he said. "Very nice." Like the rest of the flat, the room was covered in a fine layer of dust. The washbasin was intact, the jug full of water. Devlin touched it with a fingertip – icy cold. "Ambient room temperature," he murmured. The towels hadn't been touched; there was no water in the bathtub. Freddie started forward, was abruptly stilled by Devlin's hand. "In my foot-steps, Constable. Walk only where I walk."

"I didn't touch anything," Freddie protested.

"Wherever someone goes, he leaves tiny bits of himself behind," Devlin explained. "Threads from his handkerchief, the ash from his cigar, strands of hair."

"How do you know all this?" Freddie leaned over Devlin's shoulder and gazed at the w.c. with interest. "Can I pull the chain?"

"I read a lot," Devlin said. "There's a fellow in France, name of Locard. He's been making a study of it. Leave the chain alone."

"Locard?" Freddie stuck close to Devlin, nearly treading on his heels. "How do you know him?"

"The Yard occasionally has dealings with the French. I've met Monsieur Locard a few times. He runs a laboratory over there." Devlin examined the settee to no great effect and passed by the smaller of the three doors in favour of the bedroom. He tried to ignore the pounding in his chest but was unable to ignore the smell, a particular, sickly sweet fetor.

"What's that stink?" The landlady had followed them in. "Dirty bugger. He bought enough perfume for a whorehouse. How come it stinks so bad?"

"Madam, please stay back. You might want to wait on the landing," Devlin said.

"Oi! It's my bloody house and I'll do as I please!" She made to push into the room, was stopped and held by Freddie. "Who the devil are you? Explain yourself, before I get the constables round!"

"Constable Collins, kindly restrain her until I've finished my examination of the rooms," Devlin said.

"Constable?" She struggled briefly against Freddie and subsided. "What's the Yard got to do with this?"

Devlin moved further into the flat. The smell was definitely stronger the closer he got to the bedroom. Even after nearly twenty years and hundreds of cases, the stink of putrefaction still made his gorge rise. The door was ajar; Devlin pushed it open with his finger. The figure on the bed lay still and unmoving: it was Nigel Pence.

"Bloody hell . . . Collins!"

The constable appeared behind him. "Lord love a duck," he murmured. Pence had been garrotted; the line was still embedded in his neck, the two ends crossed behind the head. He had been arranged on the bed in characteristic burial pose, with his hands resting on his chest. His eyes were wide open and unseeing; Freddie couldn't stop looking at him. "No wonder he hasn't been at work. How long has he been dead?"

Devlin retrieved the cord gingerly. "I'd say three or four days, rough estimate." He coiled the garotte and dropped it into a paper sack. Something about Pence's dead face bothered him, but he couldn't pinpoint what it was. "Mrs . . . what is your name?"

"Delia Higgenbottom," she said.

"Mrs Higgenbottom, have you got a telephone about the premises?"

She drew herself up. "I have not. Wouldn't keep one of them filthy things if you paid me."

"Collins, run down to the chemist's shop and ring the Yard. I want at least four constables to secure this scene." Devlin flipped open his notebook and began jotting a rough sketch of the body, forcing his mind away from the horror of Pence's death and on to the work at hand. "Please don't touch anything, Mrs Higgenbottom."

"He's not even my lodger," she said. "I've never seen him before."

"Constable, please escort Mrs Higgenbottom downstairs. Madam, I'll want to ask you a few questions before I leave."

He crossed the room and yanked open the drapes, illuminating the room. The extra light revealed nothing new: the newspapers were still stacked in front of the fireplace, the plate of rotting food was next to the settee, and the turkey rug was . . . quite filthy, really. Devlin drew a brief sketch of the room for later reference and was about to leave when the smaller of the three doors drew his attention. Perhaps the smaller door led to a storage cupboard. Delia Higgenbottom had said Whittaker had purchased enough perfume for a whorehouse, in which case he'd have to dispose of the bottles somewhere. It was odd where Whittaker was getting the money, since his father had cut him off, but perhaps he really had made his fortune in the gold mines in Australia.

Devlin turned the handle but the door was warped. He set his foot against the wall and tugged.

The cupboard was filled, floor to ceiling, with empty glass bottles – the same glass bottles used by the chemist's shop as containers for the gentlemen's cologne called L'Aventure.

* * *

Harker was in the bathtub when Devlin arrived later that same day, fresh from the scene of Nigel Pence's murder. He'd left Freddie behind to supervise the constables and make sure no one carried off any souvenirs from the crime scene.

Harker directed Devlin to take a seat upon the closed lid of the commode, the better to converse with him. "I've come on business, Mr Harker, official police matters, you might say." Devlin wriggled a little on the lid; the hard wooden circle was pressing into his buttocks and causing him discomfort.

"Official police business?" The solicitor soaped his armpits with rather more vigour than was necessary. "Have you come to arrest me, Inspector?"

"Dennis Dalziel."

Harker's eyes widened for a moment. "Yes."

"You had been keeping company with Mr Dalziel of late."

Harker paused to dump a jug of water over his head, sputtered and gasped for some moments. "Oh no, Devlin, there your intuition has led you wrong. I was not keeping company with Dalziel for any other purpose than my current line of inquiry."

"Then what were you doing in the Peacock Club, and why the devil did you show up at the very spot where he had been murdered?"

"I habitually frequent that very shop for certain of my personal needs." Harker stood up abruptly, in a shower of droplets, and reached out a long arm for his bath sheet. Devlin tactfully looked away, occupied himself with examining the cracks in the ceiling. "I was in the Peacock Club for the purposes of an investigation. I will admit, seeing Mr

Dalziel . . . I was quite shocked." Harker hovered impatiently in the doorway.

"What investigation?" Devlin accepted the cup of hot lemon and whisky that Harker passed to him and sank into a chair beside the fire. His entire body ached, and, as usual, he hadn't been getting more than three hours of sleep at night. He wondered if he would ever sleep again. "What line of inquiry?" The hot drink warmed him through, and he felt a dangerous lassitude creeping upon him, relaxing all his limbs.

"You were at school with John Whittaker." Harker offered Devlin a cigar, lit it for him with a glowing splint from the fire.

"How d'you know that?"

Harker's features arranged themselves into an appropriately condescending expression. "Devlin."

"Yes, I was. That is to say, I knew him." Devlin waited to be struck by lightning, but some moments passed and his skin remained unsizzled.

"Your parents did without a very great deal in order to afford your tuition. They wanted to send you to a good school, give you the education they felt you deserved."

Devlin nodded. "My father was a police detective."

Harker smiled faintly and drew on his cigar. "How well did you know John Whittaker?"

Panic descended, smothering and absolute. "What do you mean?" He fancied that Harker could see right through his skin and deep into his bones, into the core and marrow of him. He could not confide in Harker; the truth was far too shattering for him to tell anyone. He preferred to leave the past right where it was, never mind dragging it all up again. It was a sordid business and it embarrassed him; if it ever got out, he could kiss his career goodbye . . . but perhaps that was Whittaker's intention, to discredit and ruin him.

"We have all, in our time, made errors in judgement, Devlin." Harker's hand reached out, closed around his wrist gently. "I would never condemn you for that." Of course, Harker would say something like that, knowing what he was, knowing the "arrangement" (when had Devlin begun to think in euphemisms?) he had with Donnelly.

Devlin forced himself to take a few deep breaths. "I started at that particular school when I was eleven. Of course, I was the new boy and not especially liked by the others." Devlin offered Harker an embarrassed grin. "You can imagine. But none of them saw fit to . . . abuse me like Whittaker did. It was a game with him, like other lads play cricket."

"I see."

"He marked me out for it, set traps, lay in wait for me. He delighted in setting the schoolmaster against me, and the other boys." Devlin picked at a hangnail on his thumb. "But I was tougher than he expected. I wouldn't have survived it, otherwise."

Harker smiled thinly. "Ah yes, Devlin, I expect you would have. We all have our resources, you know." He roused himself, paced a few steps back and forth in front of the fire, and went to look out the window. "You know that John Whittaker is married."

Devlin's eyes were in danger of quitting his skull.

"Married?"

"Oh yes." Harker puffed on his cigar. "His wife is confined in Mrs Rochester's, quite against her will. The woman is no more insane than you or I, but his family's influence and power . . ." He shrugged elegantly. "You were in the Peacock Club."

"So?" He was still digesting the fact of Whittaker's wife. In Mrs Rochester's private asylum, of all places. It was the address of choice for wealthy Londoners with insane or inconvenient relatives: continued payment ensured near-permanent incarceration, with little hope of rescue.

Harker let the window blind drop back into place. "Many aspects of this case are clear to me, Devlin, except one."

"What?"

"Why, Phoebe Alcock, of course." Harker sat down, cast a glance across at Devlin. "I am not at all certain how she figures in this equation."

"She's the Chief Commissioner's daughter." What the hell was Harker driving at?

"She came to see you at the Yard the other day. I know this because I happened to be there, talking with one of your colleagues about a case I currently have in hand."

"You . . . went to someone else?" In spite of himself, Devlin was hurt. "Why couldn't you come to me, for God's sake?"

Harker laughed. "Good God, Devlin, anyone would think you were jealous!" He leaned forward, hands on his knees. "Are you afraid I might tell him what I know? Divulge the details to less than understanding ears? You needn't worry,

Inspector. Your colleagues, I daresay, will never suspect. And you will find that I can be as silent . . ." Harker flickered a smile. ". . . as the grave."

Harker steepled his fingers underneath his chin. "I wonder, Devlin, why you have never bothered to arrest me – considering that you are privy to the most sensitive of secrets."

Devlin stammered something about the privilege of long association, confessed to turning a blind eye, consideration for one's friends, surely Mr Harker understood. "And anyway," he conceded, "if I had to arrest people for open defiance of the Act, half of bloody London would be rotting in Reading Gaol!"

Harker's eyebrows rose. "And what about you?" he asked.

Devlin stood up. "If you're making an insinuation, Mr Harker, come out with it. Otherwise, I have considerable work to do."

Harker smiled thinly. "And yet you stand here and bandy words with me. How very odd."

"Go to hell." Devlin clutched his overcoat around him and tore off out the door, his insides seething with unspent rage. He heard a rattle on the stairs above him, sensed Harker peering down on him – but the solicitor did not speak and Devlin did not look up.

* * *

Devlin found his mind returning again and again to John Whittaker's wife. Harker had not been forthcoming with his information, but that in itself was not surprising. Devlin had engaged in the long-standing game of one-upmanship with

Harker for as long as he'd known him. Perhaps it wasn't just that, though. Perhaps Harker was as much in the dark as Devlin himself, but it wouldn't be the first time that Harker had deliberately withheld information, and it certainly wouldn't be the last. He considered going back to Fowler Street, but it was getting late, and he was cold and very hungry. If he went back to the Yard, there would likely be an inevitable interview with Old Brassie, who'd want to know why Devlin had made so little progress – this was an eventuality that Devlin wanted to delay for as long as possible. He would effectively inform Sir Neville when the time was right, when he'd gathered all the pertinent threads into his hand and had something to show for his efforts.

He stood for some long moments on Camden House Road and considered what his next move might be. It was getting on for dark, and the wind had freshened with an uncommon hostility, piercing Devlin's worn coat in several places. He shivered and tried to burrow further into his collar. He had no desire to go back to his empty rooms in the Brixton Road, but neither did he want to wander about the streets of London like a Romany discard. He spotted a constable and flagged him down, gave him a note to take back to Whitehall Terrace. "Tell the sergeant at the desk I'm dining at Rules." It was rather too dear for his budget, but he'd had so little cheer these past few days that a meal at Thomas Rules' former oyster bar would be just the ticket.

Most of the menu items would leave a considerable hole in his finances; when the waiter came and enquired as to his needs (with a wholly unnecessary haughtiness), Devlin

ordered Welsh rabbit and a glass of beer. While he waited for
his meal, his gaze strayed across the adjacent tables, which
were mostly occupied by couples or the odd well-bred family with their equally well-bred and well-behaved children.
Devlin had always harboured a secret soft spot for the little
ones, even though he had long ago accepted that he would
have no issue of his own. Nearest his own table was a sump-
tuously appointed banquette, occupied by two men about his
own age, obviously friends and obviously engaged in comfortable and intimate conversation. As Devlin watched, the
taller of the two reached out and covered the other man's
hand with his own in a fleeting caress, whispering something
that Devlin could not hear. The patent evidence of warmth
and compassion was almost more than he could bear, and he
was forced to turn his eyes away.

Where was Freddie Collins tonight? Devlin found his
thoughts drifting to the young constable. For all their five
years as working partners, Devlin often felt that he knew very
little about Collins, about his habits and the company he
kept. He wondered if this reflected badly on him as a superi-
or, this lack of interest in the well-being of his subordinates
– no, that was far too pat a realisation. Freddie's life was his
own, and what he did after hours was his own business.

Devlin was halfway through coffee and a Chelsea bun
before he noticed the Bluebottle standing near the entrance.
He flagged the man, beckoning him over. "What is it, Constable . . . ?"

"Higgins, Sir. You'd best come with me right away,
Inspector."

It was yet another murder, Devlin thought – had to be, on the face of it. Nothing else would turn his guts to water like the intuition that Whittaker had struck again.

He tossed some coins upon the table and, shrugging into his overcoat, followed the constable out into the night.

* * *

Freddie Collins had decided to walk home, even though the wind was cold enough to freeze the balls off a proverbial brass monkey. He wanted the cold air, and even relished it, because it helped to clear his head and give his thoughts a more rational framework. In his agitation he'd left Devlin's office tidier than it had been in a long time and filed all the bits of stray paperwork that Devlin was wont to overlook. He'd even washed Devlin's teacup and cleaned the sticky rings from the top of the inspector's desk.

He was nearly at the entrance to his street when he heard the cries and turned instinctively to see what was the matter: an old man with severely bandy legs and the demeanour of a beggar was being hounded by three other men, all of them young and obviously fit. "Oi!" Freddie started off towards them. "What's this, then?" They predictably scattered and ran, escaping down a narrow lane between two buildings, and it occurred to Freddie that something might be amiss when he realised that the crippled man was running with them.

He stopped, began to back away and turned to make good his escape, but his way was barred by the crippled man, who had seemingly regained his health and was holding what looked to be a length of piping. Freddie reached to make the collar, but his wrists were grabbed, cinched behind him and tied with rope. He fought to stay upright on his feet, but they were too many.

They swarmed to cover him, striking out with feet and fists, until he went down under a flurry of blows. He rolled from side to side, seeking escape from the endless assaults, but could make no headway. He tasted blood inside his mouth, and a wave of dizziness threatened him, then crested and washed over him, as everything went black.

* * *

"What do you make of it, Sir?"

Devlin realised that if he'd got a fiver for every time someone had said that to him in recent days, he'd be set up for a holiday on the Continent. Devlin had never had a holiday, unless one counted the time he had accompanied his mother to the home of an aged aunt in Manchester, some years before, and Devlin was loath to count it, seeing as how he'd spent the entire time having his cheeks pinched and enduring remarks about the state of his bowels.

"He's not burned it this time." In point of fact, the dead body was astonishingly clean of effluent and blood, his own or anybody else's. Devlin mused on this for a moment, bending low over the corpse. "That's interesting." What the devil was Whittaker playing at? He'd dumped his latest on the front steps of Scotland Yard but the body was relatively untouched. "It's very interesting. You see, Constable, a killer like Whittaker has a certain list of grotesqueries he likes to enact upon his victims. In his case, he douses them with something flammable and sets them on fire." He gestured at their surroundings. "But bodies don't burn easily, and in an open area like this, with the wind blowing . . . ? He's not covering anything up, and these little bonfires of his don't destroy distinguishing features."

"Maybe . . ." The constable chewed on the end of his pencil. "Maybe this Whittaker bloke didn't kill this one. Maybe it were someone copying him, like. Or maybe he didn't light the fire, right, because he knew it would go out."

Devlin gave him a pitying look and laid an avuncular hand on the young man's shoulder. "I know Whittaker," he said, "We were at school together. As a young lad he enjoyed inflicting pain on lesser creatures: kicking the cat, picking the wings off flies." Holding a knife to a younger boy's throat and pressing until the blood came, just for fun.

The officer slid out from under Devlin's restraining arm and stood carefully to one side. "Of course, Sir."

The physiognomy of the victim intrigued Devlin: from a distance, he might pass for Freddie Collins. "How long has he – it – been here?"

The constable consulted his notebook. "I came on duty around about half-seven, Sir. It weren't here then. Me and Duffett . . ." The constable gestured at another of his ilk, standing off to the side and vomiting quietly on to his boots. ". . . came on duty about eight, Sir. It was really dark, and I went back inside to get a couple of bull's-eyes. When I came out, there he was."

"Where was Constable Collins?" He trod a careful path around the body, his eyes on the ground. Nothing to indicate that the murderer had even tried a burn and no detectable blood, so the victim had most likely been killed elsewhere.

"Sergeant Hubble said he left about half-six, Sir. Said he was going home to get some supper."

Devlin turned this over in his mind and decided to leave Freddie out of it, at least for the moment. "All right," he said, "Fetch the police surgeon." Already the curious had begun to gather round the steps, peering at the dead man with rather too much vicarious pleasure for Devlin's taste. "And get these people out of here!"

He heard the constables' cries of "Move along, there – move along, now!" only faintly. He took out his penknife and knelt beside the corpse. The body was in the early stages of rigor, a deceptive stiffness that would dissipate in a matter of hours. Devlin grunted as he flexed the arm; the dead man's hand slapped his cheek, the fingernails scratching his skin. He scrubbed his face in the shoulder of his coat and studiously ignored his own revulsion. He examined the fingernails: relatively short, meticulously manicured and clogged with a caked brown substance that might be blood and tissue or could simply be dirt. He scraped it out with his knife and took it anyway.

Devlin found Sir Neville Alcock still in his office, bent studiously over a file folder, his great girth supported against the edge of the desk. For some long moments, the Chief appeared not to see him, and so Devlin cleared his throat, rather more noisily than was necessary.

"You've been stood there for five minutes – you can manage to stand there for a few seconds more." Alcock didn't even raise his eyes from the folder, and Devlin took this as a very bad sign indeed. By the end of the interview, he supposed, he would most likely be directing omnibus traffic in Piccadilly Circus.

"I expect you've seen it," Devlin began, once he had gained the older man's attention.

"Of course I've seen it," Alcock grunted. "I'd have to be blind not to have seen it!" He heaved his bulk up out of the chair and began a slow circuit around the office, his steps as ponderous as any circus elephant and just as capable of devastation. He stopped before Devlin and gazed for some moments into the inspector's tiepin. "But it's not your fault."

Too bloody generous, Devlin thought sourly, *considering I was nowhere near.*

"He means to send a message to us, this Whittaker. Means to take us down a notch, draw the ire of the public and the press, make fools of us."

"I found something under the fingernails that might be blood. The victim," Devlin said, "perhaps he scratched Whittaker."

Alcock grunted. "And perhaps he scratched his own arse," he said. "How long since you've been home, Devlin?"

Devlin's mouth opened and closed on nothing.

"How long since you've had a good night's sleep? Eh? Don't think I haven't noticed. Good night's sleep just the thing for you. Young chaps of your sort haven't got the stamina that we used to have. You need to get a good meal in you."

This was something, Devlin thought, coming from a man

who looked as if he routinely devoured a hog each dinner-time.

"Go home, Devlin." Alcock turned his back, effectively dismissing him. "Get some sleep and come back here with some concrete ideas on how to catch this fellow Whittaker." He turned and bellowed at Devlin, in a voice loud enough to carry all the way to Essex, "And find yourself a woman!"

* * *

It wasn't that Devlin found himself a woman so much as a woman found him. He was awakened out of sleep by Mrs Taylor, bending over him and rolling him to and fro, hissing in his ear that a gentleman was here to see him and hadn't he best get up and receive his visitor?

"For God's sake!" Devlin rolled over and opened one eye. "Who is it, at this time of night?"

"Don't take that tone with me!" Mrs Taylor, ever resourceful, and quite used by now to dealing with the inspector, wrung one of his ears until he yelped. "A young man, very handsome, nicely dressed. He's got lovely manners. You'd best see him."

"Go away," Devlin moaned. But he got up anyway and shrugged into his dressing gown, the better to receive John Donnelly.

The chemist made no preamble: "Freddie Collins is very badly hurt. I came here as soon as I found out." He reached out to steady Devlin, hold him upright. "You're shivering – here." Donnelly fetched a blanket from the sofa and wrapped it around Devlin, who felt as if he'd been drenched in icy water.

"What happened?" Devlin asked, and then, "What time is it?"

"Just past midnight. As far as we can tell, he was attacked on his way home, lured into a laneway."

"How did you find out?" He'd have been alone, Devlin thought, and likely preoccupied with other matters, as he often was.

"Harker is also working toward a resolution of this case." Donnelly sloshed some brandy into a glass and handed it across to the inspector. "He asked that I relay the information to you."

"I should have known Harker would be involved!" Devlin gulped the brandy hastily, his mind already running ahead. "Where is Freddie? Is he in the hospital?"

"He's recuperating at a safe location. Harker thought it unwise to allow him to linger in a public hospital."

"Harker! What right has Harker to decide?" Devlin tossed the blanket off his shoulders, went through to the bedroom and began dressing as hastily as his shivering would allow. "Fowler Street," he said. "Take me there."

Donnelly caught the inspector by the forearms, stilled his headlong flight. "He's not at Fowler Street."

"Then where the bloody hell have you put him?"

"Get into your coat and come with me." Donnelly gathered up Devlin's hat and gloves. "There's a cab at the door."

* * *

Freddie had never felt so bad in his life. He was lying in a nice bed, very comfortable, but he felt as though someone had tried to turn him inside out. Thank God for Donnelly, who at least had offered something for the pain, something which eased the savage grip of his injuries. The only downside was that it tended to make him astonishingly sleepy and to produce bizarre and varied dreams, not unlike the visions of Samuel Taylor Coleridge, with whose work Freddie had a nodding acquaintance.

In his more lucid moments, he worried about Devlin and whether Whittaker was even now stalking the inspector with an eye to murdering him, now that Freddie had been taken out of the way. Perhaps it had been Whittaker in the archives room that morning and perhaps he had deliberately infiltrated the offices of the Yard to weaken their resolve, to torment them with lingering and unfounded suppositions. Privately, he fingered these theories over in his mind, but he knew that he would never mention any of this to Devlin. Freddie had a deathly fear of seeming stupid to the Guv'nor, and he already suspected that Devlin thought him a little dim. He didn't want to lower the inspector's opinion of him by offering theories that might ultimately prove disappointing.

"How much further?" Devlin bit hard on his lower lip, quashing an urge to pummel Donnelly with his fists. After all, it wasn't the chemist's fault that he was overwrought and tortured with worry.

"Not long now." Donnelly reached out and patted Devlin's arm in the darkness of the cab. "He is being well cared for, Devlin. Ah, here we are."

The cabbie had stopped in front of a nondescript brownstone in Kensington, the sort of address usually occupied by those whose financial means did not outweigh their taste. Devlin disembarked and followed Donnelly into the house, stumbling on the steps in his haste, half blind and dizzy with fatigue. "Easy, Inspector." Donnelly wrapped an arm around his waist and ushered him into the foyer, where Violet Pearson, dressed in silk pajamas and a smoking jacket (in deference to the hour), met them. Her long red hair was unbound and flowed freely round her shoulders; she was, Devlin thought, an uncommonly handsome woman.

"Inspector Devlin!" She took Devlin's hands in hers and gave them a gentle squeeze. "You must be half out of your wits with worry! Right this way." She led him up a narrow staircase and along the upstairs hall, pausing outside one of the bedrooms. "Donnelly has administered laudanum for the pain, so Constable Collins might well be sleeping."

Devlin reached for the doorknob and his courage failed him and, with it, the last of his strength. He slid down the wall to end up in an awkward sitting position with his overcoat bunched around his knees. "Oh my God," he whispered, thankful that only Mrs Pearson was present to see his complete breakdown. "How bad is it?"

She knelt before him, her hands on his knees. "It looks rather worse than it actually is, or so Mr Donnelly tells me." She smoothed his cheek with the back of her knuckles and smiled. "You must take courage, Inspector! Constable Collins needs your strength now." She helped him to his feet, leaned in and kissed his cheek. "Go in and satisfy yourself, Inspector, with the knowledge that your constable will indeed recover. Of that much I am certain."

Devlin waited till her footsteps had retreated down the stairs before venturing into the bedroom. The lamp had been turned down to a mere flicker in the darkness, and Devlin was loath to tamper with it for fear of waking Freddie. He drew near to the bed in which the young constable lay sleeping, reached out to touch one of Freddie's hands, cradling the limp fingers against his palm as he sank into a chair. He forced himself to look, to assess and catalogue the damage: random bruising on the face and a nasty cut above one eye that had swollen and puffed to astonishing proportions. Devlin sighed, drew the covers back from Freddie's naked torso. They had been at him with fists and feet; Devlin traced the map of bruises with his gaze, not daring to touch Freddie for fear of causing him more pain than had already been endured. He saw what looked like puncture marks from hobnailed boots along the young man's sides, and further down his thighs; it was clear that more than one man had provoked and sustained this. Devlin vowed that he would scour the bowels of London until he found them. Perhaps he wouldn't even allow them benefit of trial, he thought savagely, perhaps he'd kill them all himself, with just his bare hands and perhaps a pair of hobnailed boots.

"Sir."

"Shhh . . . don't try to talk." Devlin had sworn he would not weep, but his tears burned his face like vitriol. "I came as soon as I heard."

"I've been stupid, haven't I?" Freddie's grip tightened on Devlin's fingers. "Didn't keep my head down like you taught me, went charging in like a bloody maniac."

"Collins . . ." Devlin pressed his lips to the young man's palm, the one place on his body that remained undamaged. "So help me God, I'll find them. I'll find them and I'll deal with them, supposing I swing for it!"

Freddie freed his hand and pressed his fingers against Devlin's mouth, shushing him. "Not your fault."

"Of course it's my bloody fault." He knew Whittaker, knew the things Whittaker would do to him and anybody close to him. He was surprised Whittaker had waited this long to attack Freddie.

"Did you see them?" Devlin asked. "Could you identify them if you saw them again?"

"They weren't anybody special," Freddie said quietly. "Bludgers, footpads, you know the type," and then, "Phoebe told me everything." A slight smile played about his lips; he was no longer making any sense. Freddie hardly scintillated at the best of times, but under the thrall of laudanum he was completely unintelligible.

Devlin smiled fondly at him. "Phoebe?"

"A woman on your arm is the best camouflage, Sir. Even Mr Harker thinks so." Freddie's fingers caught hold of Devlin's sleeve. "Mr Harker's right, you know."

Devlin snorted. "Mr Harker! As if Mr Harker would know a woman from his watch chain!"

But Freddie was already too far sunk in sleep to hear him, and finally, Devlin crept quietly from the room.

* * *

"Phillip." Phoebe hugged him tightly, took both his

hands in hers. "Violet has made tea. Please come and sit with us." Her eyes were preternaturally bright, glittering and predatory. *Say nothing,* her smile said, *because I have the means to destroy you.*

Devlin perceived Donnelly sitting near the fire, devouring the largest Chelsea bun that Devlin had ever seen. At Devlin's approach, the apothecary looked up and mumbled something through a mouthful of pastry, then buried his face in his teacup.

"Thank you." Devlin took the cup and saucer, but declined a Chelsea bun. His stomach felt as if some Yorkshire codger had used it for a round of ferret-legging.

"Violet was telling me that Constable Collins might do better if he stayed with us for the duration of his recovery." Phoebe glanced across at Violet, now semi-recumbent on a chaise longue and smoking a cigarette in a long ivory holder. "This is a most discreet household, and Violet and I can provide for most of Constable Collins's needs right here. With assistance from Mr Donnelly, of course."

Intellectually, Devlin knew that she was right, although he feared to have Freddie languish under any protection but his own. "I expect you're right," he allowed reluctantly. He wondered how he might go about his daily duties, knowing that Freddie was the recuperative hostage of two tribades in a brownstone house in Kensington.

"We'll take good care of him," Violet interjected. "He will want for nothing. Phoebe and I will care for him as though he were a much-beloved brother." She smiled as Phoebe came to stand behind her, a hand upon the redhead's shoulder. "As far as this Whittaker is concerned, Freddie will appear to have vanished from the planet."

Devlin laid his teacup down. "It's not Freddie that he's interested in." He held his tired, aching head between his palms. "I think he's after me."

Donnelly started, his teacup clanking in the saucer. "Good heavens, whatever for? What have you done to him that he needs to seek this kind of vengeance?"

Devlin laughed mirthlessly. "A long and sordid tale, Mr Donnelly."

Violet Pearson cast a curiously assessing gaze at him. "I expect Whittaker didn't take too kindly to your throwing him over, all those years ago."

Devlin would have reacted, except his nerves had long ago surrendered. "Who told you?" he asked, his fatigue lending a deceptive mildness to the query.

Violet shrugged, an elegant lifting of her slender shoulders under the smoking jacket. "We each have our histories, Inspector."

Devlin stood up to go. "Well, be that as it may, I do have a murderer to catch and other business to attend to before this is all tied up." He laid the cup and saucer on a side table. "Ladies, thank you for the tea. Mr Donnelly, your presence has been most helpful."

"Where are you going?" Phoebe started forward, tugging at his sleeve. "Surely you're not going out after this Whittaker again, at this hour?"

"Surely I am, Miss Alcock, and 'this Whittaker' as you are wont to call him, is not likely to wait upon my pleasure before he kills again." Devlin shoved his hands into his gloves. "He will be planning his next move, and we must anticipate him." Quite the opposite: if Whittaker saw his target in view, he'd strike at once. He preferred his gratification to be immediate and thorough.

"Inspector Devlin, if I may be so bold, you are exhausted, Sir!" Violet Pearson rose from the chaise longue like a cat uncoiling itself and shook her long hair out. "Why not stay here till the morning? We are only too happy to provide you with a bed."

"Because I must make my way to Fowler Street," Devlin replied. "It's time Mr Harker and I joined forces, whether it's to our mutual benefit or not."

Donnelly roused himself. "Devlin, if you like, I can come with you."

Devlin considered it for a moment, then waved it away. "No, but thank you. Perhaps you might remain to care for Freddie. I'm sure you can do the most good here, where you're needed." Besides which, he told himself, it was necessary that he speak to Harker alone, without Donnelly's mitigating influence.

* * *

"Sarah Whittaker." Devlin didn't bother to sit down, this not being a social call. Besides, he knew that if he sank into one of Harker's comfortable chairs, he would be asleep in moments. He couldn't remember the last time he'd had a proper rest, a good night's sleep where no one bothered him and no one woke him prematurely to tell him something he didn't care to know. His eyelids felt gritty and a muscle in his cheek had begun to twitch. If this were any other case, he'd force himself to take a rest, get a decent meal, but this wasn't, and he couldn't remember the last time he'd eaten anything larger than a sandwich. The Welsh rabbit at the restaurant – that was about it.

"Do sit down," Harker said. "I'd rather you didn't fall unconscious on the turkey rug. We've only just had it cleaned." He pushed Devlin into a chair and rang for tea and "at least a sandwich, Inspector, for I perceive you've taken little nourishment today". He fixed Devlin with his eagle eye. "Now, how is young Collins?"

Devlin goggled at him. "How the devil . . . ?"

Harker waved it away. "You did right to leave him with the women. Yes, the gentler sex is possessed of an innate desire to help mankind."

"He . . . it's very bad. A gang of them, certainly, perhaps as many as four or five." Devlin swallowed hard. He became keenly aware of his own hands – lean, tense – turning his hat round and round.

"And you suspect Whittaker?"

But Devlin's reply was curtailed by Harker's landlady, Mrs Cadogan, bearing a laden tea tray with fresh bread and cold meats, golden scones and jam and clotted Devon cream. Harker bade him pull in to the table, and Devlin stuffed himself while they talked desultorily about the details of the case. When the teapot was empty and the last of the scones had disappeared, Devlin sat back in his chair, wondering vaguely if his trouser buttons could stand the strain of his full belly. He accepted a cigar from Harker and lit it. "I neglected to mention Nigel Pence."

Harker puffed at his own Cuban with every appearance of enjoyment. "The laboratory attendant."

"Mr Harker, is there anything you don't know?"

"Not that I'm aware of, Inspector."

"We found him murdered, in lodgings that might have belonged to Whittaker." Devlin fought to keep a note of exasperation out of his voice: how was he expected to carry out an investigation with Reginald Harker for ever twenty steps in front of him?

"Might have belonged to him?"

"I found Whittaker's sleeve links there, the same ones he wore at school." The cigar tasted like old ashes in his mouth; he stubbed it out in the ashtray. "It's Elizabeth Hobbs all over again. Yes, I made a right job of that one, and all." He rested his head in his hand. Perhaps it might be good to rest for a moment, just close his eyes . . .

Someone was drawing a blanket over him, and he fought it, clawing at the obstruction, seeking to remove it . . . he couldn't let them draw the sheet over his face, because he wasn't dead yet and wouldn't be for a long time.

"Devlin, lie still." Harker's voice came to him in the half-light, warmer and more comforting than Devlin would ever have thought possible. "You would think I was trying to smother you." The solicitor drew the blankets round him and turned to blow out the lamp. Devlin felt his body compress the mattress as Harker turned over and sighed.

"Remind me to tell you about Sarah Whittaker."

"Sarah Whittaker." Devlin was floating in warmth, absolutely safe and comfortable. Harker's bed was made of jelly, soft and eminently pliable, and he was sinking into it, as boneless as an eel.

"John Whittaker's wife." Harker paused for so long that Devlin wondered if the solicitor had drifted into sleep, but Harker was merely yawning. "We shall see her tomorrow."

Devlin asked the question he'd been waiting to ask all night. "Will you help me?" He could just make out Harker's features in the gloom, the pale glow of his face and his white nightshirt.

"Of course." Harker smiled at him. "But sleep now, my dear Inspector, for I see you are desperately in need of it."

Devlin went out like a blown candle.

CHAPTER EIGHT

BERTHA ROCHESTER'S PRIVATE lunatic asylum never failed to depress Devlin to the uttermost. During the course of his duties as a constable and later, as a police inspector, he had often had cause to visit, and he always came away from these visits feeling rather more depressed than when he'd gone. There was just something about the dim, grey building and its dim, grey inhabitants that seemed to drain the life out of him and instill in him a sense of over-whelming hopelessness.

He and Harker had arisen early this morning, breakfast-ed upon an excellent repast prepared by Mrs Cadogan and taken a cab to Mrs Rochester's, hoping to find Mrs Sarah Whittaker. The morning was overcast and cool and the air tasted like rain; in another month it would be snow, but with any luck Whittaker would be caught and Devlin could worry about something else for a change.

"Did you sleep well last night, Devlin?" Harker climbed into the cab briskly, tucked his long legs against the seat.

"I did," Devlin said. "Mr Harker, I feel I should thank you."

Harker lifted one elegantly gloved hand. "Ah, Devlin, even the most austere of us is prey to creature comforts." The solicitor was in one of his expansive moods this morning, Devlin thought. Doubtless it had something to do with the quarry which they were seeking. Harker was practically quivering with anticipation. "You know, I often find that there's nothing like proper rest and adequate nourishment to prepare one for the work at hand. I completely understand why Donnelly so constantly bullies me to eat, you know."

"He didn't come home last night?" Devlin wondered if his presence had perhaps driven a wedge between Harker and the chemist.

"He sent word by messenger that he would remain with Constable Collins. Miss Alcock and Mrs Pearson were quite insistent that he accept their hospitality." Harker said nothing about Freddie, and Devlin wondered if the solicitor thought to shield him. Perhaps Whittaker's thugs (if they were in fact in his employ, and not merely street ruffians as Freddie supposed) had done more damage than originally thought. After all, Donnelly wasn't a doctor and thus wouldn't know the true extent of Freddie's injuries. Perhaps Donnelly had stayed because Freddie had taken a turn for the worse?

Harker stiffened to attention. "Ah – we're here!" The cab juddered to a stop and he leapt out with Devlin hard on his heels, and it wasn't until Devlin had ascended some several steps that he realised the cabbie was still waiting (with rather ill grace) for payment.

"Ah . . ." Devlin fumbled in his pockets, counted coins into his hand. "I think that should do it, Cabbie. Thank you."

The man looked disdainfully at Devlin's offering, wondering why coppers were so bloody cheap and how come he hadn't got a tip. He ought to take his cab and go across the Channel to the Frogs. At least they knew how to express appreciation. "You're all heart, Guv'nor." The cabbie jingled the coins in his hand.

Devlin caught up with Harker just inside the door. The solicitor was leaning against the wall, feigning nonchalance, but Devlin could detect something rather uneasy in his air of studied carelessness, the way he flicked his walking stick rather nervously against first one shoulder, then the other. Nursing sisters hurried here and there, some balancing trays with medicines, and Devlin saw a burly orderly go by with what appeared to be an oversized leather dog collar. "I expect she's on the wards," Devlin said.

Harker, gazing steadily before him, saw nothing.

"Mr Harker?" Devlin touched the solicitor's arm. "Are you all right?"

Harker seemed to pull himself back from some precipice and straightened abruptly. "Devlin! What are we standing here for? We have work!"

Devlin followed as Harker led the way down the dimly lit corridor, always keeping to the side and a little behind the solicitor, in an effective shadowing position. Devlin had little experience in dealing directly with lunatics – thankfully, his scope had been confined to flying visits and note taking – and he wasn't sure how secure the locks and bars were in this place. He'd been here not five minutes and already his skin was beginning to crawl; another five minutes in this place and he'd run gibbering into the bright October morning. He wondered how Harker could stand it: quite apart from the stench (a cross between the smell of human feces and an open sore) and the noise (from men and women crammed alike into overcrowded cells, some silent while others shrieked and howled), there was the general air of helpless desperation that seemed to corrode his soul.

Harker stopped in front of an iron door that was bolted and padlocked from the outside. "Do you see that woman?"

Devlin, standing on tiptoe to peer over Harker's shoulder, saw the crouching figure of an elderly woman. Her iron-grey hair, matted with twigs and straw, flowed unconfined over her narrow shoulders; her feet were bare, and for clothing she wore only a shredded linen shift. Her hands and face were filthy, the fingernails grown long and savage, and as she sat and watched them, she rocked back and forth on her haunches, peering at them mutely, a creature entirely untamed.

"Is it Sarah Whittaker?" Devlin asked. But this woman was old, and John Whittaker surely would have taken a woman of his own age, given his vanity for such things.

"No," Harker replied. "It is my mother."

Devlin waited while an attendant unlocked the complicated series of bolts that would admit them to Sarah Whittaker's cell. He was prepared to see just about anything,
especially now, after Harker's shocking revelation. Harker's
eccentricities aside, Devlin would have expected an elderly
society matron or even some superannuated opera hag, but a
madwoman? His own parents had never made it out of the
lower middle class, but at least they'd had the good grace to
die of something normal. The cell door swung back and they
stepped into an interior that was painted white, with a high
window that admitted some small degree of light into the
room. Someone had gone to the trouble of fixing curtains
there, and Devlin could easily discern the care that had gone
into creating the delicate embroidery and ruffled edges. Just
underneath the window was a writing desk with a selection
of pens, a blotter and an ink bottle; the chair adjacent was
draped with a scrap of discarded velvet, probably to hide its
worn and battered appearance. The room had clearly been
furnished with care; Mrs Whittaker obviously anticipated a
longer-than-average stay.

"Mr Harker." The woman on the bed rose gracefully and,
moving to where they were, reached to shake Harker's hand.
"I am so grateful you have come. Your legal counsel was
always most welcome to me in days gone by." She peered over
Harker's shoulder at Devlin. "But who is this friend of
yours?"

She was a small woman, neat and tidy, with blonde hair
coiled at the back of her head. An apron, much smudged
with various bright colours, protected her dark dress, and

Devlin realised that she'd been painting, that there was an easel in the corner of the room with a half-completed figure on it.

"Inspector Phillip Devlin, Scotland Yard, Ma'am."

She squeezed his hand warmly. "I imagine you expected to find a howling madwoman, did you not, Inspector? But I am retained here for other reasons."

"Madam, you are most gracious in agreeing to this visit." Harker gestured that she should sit down. "Inspector Devlin and I are engaged in an investigation concerning your husband."

"Ah. My husband." She nodded at Devlin, standing by the desk. "I married foolishly, Inspector, for the security of my husband's wealth and name, and not for love. We were very young. Ten years ago he emigrated to Australia. He was meant to stay there. I remember hearing some nonsense about the gold mines." She examined her fingernails, picked at a stray fleck of paint. "Less than a year after John left England he was back again. He didn't like Australia."

Devlin blinked. "And the marriage?" It was an awkward, unfortunate question, but it couldn't be helped.

"I could not satisfy him." Any other woman would have quailed at the admission, but she didn't even blink. "His tastes run in rather a different direction, Inspector, as I am sure you know." Devlin felt the prickle of sweat underneath his arms. Had she been told?

She turned to Harker. "My husband is a madman, Mr Harker, of that I have no doubt. I am not certain what has so disturbed his mind, but I hear talk that his brain is addled by disease." She smiled at Devlin. "Even in this place, we do receive some news."

"Forgive me, Madam," Devlin felt compelled to interject, "but you yourself, if I may say so, do not seem particularly mad."

Harker shot a look at the inspector. "She's not," he said. "And that's precisely why she's in here."

"My husband's family have great wealth, Inspector, and even greater influence. Whatever John wants, he tends to get. When I became inconvenient, he decided to have me put away."

"That's barbaric!"

"But not so very difficult, Inspector. All it takes are the signatures of two doctors, a sworn affidavit from each of these distinguished gentlemen declaring me incurably insane, and I am deprived of my liberty." Her lips twisted. "Two, Inspector. And yet it requires a jury of twelve to convict your average malefactor." She sat down on the bed. "A woman in my position has no voice, and few resources with which to ensure justice. She is merely an . . . addendum." She drew a slow, meditative breath. "With John loose in London, perhaps my imprisonment is a disguised blessing. I am safe here, within these walls. He cannot get to me."

Devlin nodded. "So Mr Harker . . ."

". . . is no longer qualified for the practice of the law." The solicitor finished Devlin's nascent sentence smoothly.

"Pity," said Devlin.

Harker ignored him. "Madam. We think your husband has murdered again." Harker laid this information out before her with his usual precision and economy of words. "A police constable has been ambushed and badly beaten, and members of Scotland Yard have received veiled hints that there is worse to come."

"While you might be safe, others are not," Devlin said. "We suspect him of five murders that we know of, possibly six." He didn't like to shock her, but he needed information. "Several days ago your husband sent me a severed human head in a hatbox."

"A hatbox." Her eyes widened. "That is unfortunate, Inspector, and I am sorry, but I'm afraid I can tell you nothing."

"You fear for your safety?"

"My husband's family are well connected, Inspector." Her pale hands played about the hem of her apron, pulling it towards her, pleating it and letting it drop. "I console myself that I am beyond their reach, but one never knows for certain." She paused, glanced at each of them in turn. "John was always shockingly unconventional in his behaviour. It has much to do with these friends of his."

Devlin snapped to attention. "What friends?"

"The Hell Fire Club, Inspector. Doubtless you've heard of them. Oh, many people in London nowadays think it died away at the end of the last century, but that is an erroneous assumption."

"The Hell Fire Club are a group of moneyed ruffians, Inspector, who cloak their true purpose in pageantry and silly ritual. They are quite selective about their membership, but one can be sponsored into the club if one has a father or brother in the rank and file."

"I have heard," Harker said, "that they profess to worship Satan."

"They have no need to worship Satan, Mr Harker, and if indeed that were true, it would be a far simpler explanation than any I could furnish. No, they delight in causing havoc in the lives of others, of destroying where they might. They often strike at those among society whom they deem 'unnatural'."

Devlin felt again the uneasy prickle, tried unsuccessfully to dismiss it. She was staring at him with patent resentment, a complete reversal of her earlier reticence. *I know you*, her gaze said. *I know what you are.*

"Unnatural?" he asked.

Her gaze slid away, her hands furiously pleating the apron. "Any deeds that John himself is not keen to furnish, he will have some members of that unholy brotherhood to assist him.

Harker's still posture fractured into sudden movement. "Mrs Whittaker, thank you."

They retraced their steps back through the hospital, past the howling inmates, past the stinking cells that were little more than cages. Harker stopped a nursing sister and enquired for an orderly. "Forgive me, Inspector." He nodded at the cell door. "You are not obligated to remain." Harker would never ask; he was far too proud.

"Since you agreed to accompany me, Mr Harker, I'm afraid I must. I'm responsible for your safety." Devlin assumed a deliberately bland expression. "If any harm were to come to you, I'd never hear the end of it."

Harker dipped his head slightly, a tacit acknowledgement, and then the great door swung inward. The woman was crouched in the corner as before, but with their entry she seemed to become agitated, rocking back and forth and muttering, watching them out of the corners of her eyes. "It's like a Gothic novel, isn't it?" Harker murmured. "The madwoman in the attic." He moved a little closer, and when she did not flinch away, folded himself down on to the pallet. "Mother, how are you?" Inane, as pleasantries usually were, but rendered especially poignant by Harker's desperate surroundings. "It's Reg. I've come to visit you."

She crouched in the gloom, watching them; there was a flurry of movement and Harker's sudden, anguished cry. Devlin was on his feet, pulling him backwards out of the cell. The door clanged shut; Harker was leaning against the wall, patting his face with a handkerchief. Devlin could clearly see three long, deep gouges, each rapidly filling up with blood.

"Here." Devlin applied his own handkerchief. "You'll need to get that looked at."

"Do not trouble yourself, Inspector." Harker tossed his own wadded up handkerchief at the rubbish bin; it went in. "I am quite well." He turned and walked away, his footsteps sounding crisply in the hollow corridor.

"I don't understand," Devlin confessed, as he hurtled back through London with Harker.

"What is it that you don't understand, Devlin?"

The inspector was silent. He had no right to ask, and it was none of his business in the first place.

"Doubtless you are referring to my mother."

Devlin conceded the point.

"Ah, Devlin . . . there you lead me into the realms of ancient family history." The solicitor leaned slightly forward and gazed into the inspector's dark eyes. "Your constable, young Collins – was he ever a member of the Hell Fire Club?"

"I don't believe so," Devlin said, "Freddie's from Pimlico, Mr Harker, you know that. From what I've read, these Hell Fire chaps are snobs. It's doubtful they'd let Freddie join . . . and besides, Freddie is a police officer. He would never have anything to do with that gang of reprobates."

Harker snorted. "If you only knew, Devlin – if you only knew the names of all the politicians and policemen, men of the cloth and university dons. It is true that the Hell Fire Club was initially founded on the precipitous nature of the aristocratic classes, but it has grown beyond that, much beyond that." The solicitor reflected for a moment. "Perhaps Constable Collins is secretly aristocratic."

Devlin inwardly chided himself for wanting to laugh out loud. "But why would Freddie . . . he couldn't possibly have anything in common with them." Unless Freddie really was hiding an aristo or two in his family tree . . . It would explain the idiocy. Devlin smiled thinly, his great strain evident upon his face. "It's me Whittaker is after, Mr Harker. It's me he's always been after. Freddie was just . . . convenient."

The cab shuddered to a stop in front of Scotland Yard, and as Devlin made as if to exit, he was stayed by Harker's hand. "Tell me about Elizabeth Hobbs."

Devlin blinked. "The official story is that he contracted syphilis from her."

"But no proof."

"We were never able to make him submit to the necessary medical examinations. His conviction was overturned and he fled the country."

Harker nodded.

"He killed her, Mr Harker," Devlin said. "Believe me." Ten years ago, an empty flat in Camden House Road, and Devlin fancied he could still smell the sulphurous fume of Whittaker's lit match.

Let her go.

Whittaker held the girl by the collar of her dress. The heels of her shoes were hooked over the window sash. She was crying. *I'm going to burn her like she's burned me.* It was Devlin he'd always wanted; Devlin that he had lured. *I'll kill her. And I'll make you watch.*

"Regardless of where he contracted the disease, he blamed Elizabeth Hobbs." Harker's voice broke into Devlin's thoughts.

"He set her on fire. She'd been wearing a wig."

"*Alopecia syphilitica,*" Harker said. "A hallmark of the tertiary stage." He stopped, his expression as close to bewilderment as Devlin had ever seen it. "If he's in the tertiary stage himself, he's probably bald as well. It's a very great truth, Inspector, that human beings often seek to destroy what they themselves either envy or cannot have."

It had flamed up horribly, the scent of burning protein sickening in the confined space. "And then he threw her out the window." Devlin had left her and gone after Whittaker alone; Whittaker was too quick for him, gave him the slip in a narrow lane behind a butcher's shop.

"It was my fault," Devlin said.

"What was your fault, Inspector?"

"I left her there. He gave me the slip and circled back around, did the proper job of it."

"She was already dead, Inspector." Harker's gloved hand rested for a moment on his forearm. "I am certain we will find him."

"Perhaps, Mr Harker." Devlin stepped down from the cab, leaning into the darkness of its interior. "Before he does it again." She had screamed all the way down, but it was just a short drop, really, just a step out of an upstairs window. The burned wig floated away on the wind. Devlin chased him the length and breadth of the East End, without effect. And in the end Whittaker had gotten away with it.

"Devlin, these are indeed murky waters." Harker sighed. "Will you have supper with me some evening this week?"

Devlin stepped back from the cab. "Only if you're paying."

"If Whittaker is not taken into custody very soon, Devlin, I fancy we shall all be paying."

Harker tapped his walking stick against the cab's interior, and drove away.

* * *

It was strange for Devlin that he was at his desk without Freddie Collins hovering around. He hadn't realised how much he depended on Collins until the young constable had been so brutally taken out of commission. Quite apart from the fact that he had to fetch his own tea (a task that Devlin loathed, because it took him past the ubiquitous clutch of sergeants lounging in the downstairs hallway), he missed Freddie's steadying presence. Meanwhile, there still remained Nigel Pence's garrotte and the note that the now deceased medical student had taken out of Chimpy Darwin's ear. Devlin spread it out on the desk carefully and examined it with his magnifier. There was nothing special about it: the note had been written on regular, garden-variety paper, available from any one of a hundred stationers in London. The writing, oddly enough, was in pencil – a particularly greasy pencil, considering that Chimpy Darwin's blood and fluids hadn't caused the lettering to degrade. The fact that the note had been rolled up instead of folded had also helped to preserve the message.

I am Down on whores and I shan't quit ripping them till I do get buckled.

There was no signature; the writing slanted backwards at an extreme angle, and in several spots the writer had pressed quite hard on his pencil, leaving indentations in the paper that were visible from the back. Why quote Jack the Ripper? Why not enlist some sentiment of one's own? The note that came with the hatbox had been specific, alluding to the "gifts" the murderer had left, but this message was generic, quite unremarkable. It could have been written by anyone.

Devlin went very still. He laid his palms on the desk and forced himself to breathe.

What had Nigel Pence been doing in that flat? Had he decided to go after Whittaker himself? Not likely, since it wasn't exactly his purview, but Devlin's. The landlady had denied ever seeing Pence before, yet she had a good enough recollection of "the toff" who'd rented her rooms. How had Pence gotten past her? Devlin's own landlady, Mrs Taylor, never missed a trick; if Devlin had been in the habit of bringing strange young gentlemen home to his rooms, Mrs Taylor would know about it. Perhaps Pence was a confederate, someone to do the dirty work for Whittaker?

He turned from his contemplation as the door creaked open and Phoebe Alcock peered inside. Today she was wearing a very handsome green walking dress, with a matching hat that brought out the lambent green accents in her warm hazel eyes. "Is this a bad time?"

Devlin felt some of his anger recede. "No, Phoebe, of course not – please, come in." He arranged a chair for her and waited while she sat down. "Let me get you some tea."

"The tea can wait." Phoebe dimpled at him over the desk. "You and I have work to do, Inspector, and I've gotten Father's express permission to steal you for an hour."

"Phoebe, I can't just up and leave. I've got work to do."

She would not accept his refusal on any terms. She was on strict orders, she said, from Violet Pearson, to ensure that Devlin received his daily quota of fresh air. Devlin wondered peevishly if his daily quota included the oxygenic contents of a private lunatic asylum.

"Freddie is doing much better." Phoebe tightened her grip on his arm and smiled up at him. "Mr Donnelly has been caring for him night and day – you'd think he was a doctor, the way he goes on about this or that medicine. Of course, he is absolutely relentless in his fussing and fretting, your young constable. Keeps asking when he can go back on duty."

"I've had another letter from Whittaker." Devlin wondered if he should divulge the contents, and then remembered that this was the woman on whom his entire future depended. "He makes reference to whores." He tilted a glance at Phoebe. "I can't understand it. He's only ever murdered one whore, Elizabeth Hobbs. This puerile attempt at mockery makes no sense that I can see."

"Well . . ." Phoebe thought for a moment. "I think you're coming at it from a strictly male point of view, Phillip."

Devlin wondered exactly when she'd decided to drop the "Inspector".

"Oh?"

"A woman would immediately understand the reference, because she knows that the suspicion of improper behaviour at any level brings with it the label of 'whore'." Phoebe steered him, by a pressure of her hand, into the park. "Someone who's had a dalliance, someone who has perhaps brought an intimate shame upon the aggressor."

"Not necessarily a woman, in that case," Devlin observed.

"Quite so." Phoebe drew him down on to a bench. "Now," she said, "when are you going to kiss me?"

Devlin blinked at her, suddenly embarrassed, as Phoebe drew his face to hers and kissed him gently, with an excess of tenderness, upon the mouth. In the midst of this caress, Devlin experienced the sort of bizarre epiphany that so often marked his habits, and sprang up off the bench as though an electrical wire had been surreptitiously applied to his hindquarters.

"Whores!" he cried, seizing Phoebe's hands in his and drawing her into an ecstatic hug. "Whores, Miss Alcock! Whores of any stripe!"

A group of strollers walking *en famille* bent evil glances in Devlin's direction, and Phoebe felt compelled to clamp her palm over his mouth to prevent any further likewise eruptions. "A whore," she said quietly, "is not necessarily a woman."

He felt something loosening inside of him as the terrible tension began to dissipate. Here, then, was a thread upon which he might reasonably fasten his hopes. "Phoebe," he cried, "I adore you!"

"Then marry me."

Her gaze was solemn and steadfast; Devlin saw that she could not possibly be joking. All at once, the gentle autumn sky seemed something other than banal, and long-forgotten debts came whistling on the winds.

"Sorry?"

"Marry me, Inspector." She took his arm, drew him with her on to the path. "A marriage in name only, but sufficient to secure both our reputations."

She was upping the stakes, Devlin realised. He could not imagine going to Sir Neville and announcing that he wished for Phoebe's hand in marriage. Old Brassie would probably open up his massive jaws and swallow Devlin whole.

"Father has already given his consent, if that's what you're wondering about."

Devlin drew a hand over his face, "I daresay you wasted no time, once I'd agreed to your initial conditions." She had him by the short hairs, and there was nothing he could do about it. All she had to do was make his letters known and his career was finished. "I am curious about one thing: where did you get my letters? Who gave them to you?"

She pulled away from him, drifted over to a stand of trees, now gloriously in autumn colour. Her handkerchief was clutched in her hand, and to an onlooker it would appear that she was crying. Devlin knew otherwise.

"Please." She appealed to him, "It would make everything so much simpler, for both of us."

"It would make things simpler for you, perhaps. No doubt your father would be relieved." Devlin moved to look at her. "And where does it leave me?" he murmured. "You've apprised me of your feelings for Mrs Pearson and that the two of you plan to go abroad together? Tell me, Phoebe: where would I fit, in such an arrangement?"

She scrubbed at her eyes angrily with the back of her hand. "This isn't easy for me, you know. A man has a certain autonomy, can move about in the world unhindered, where- as a woman . . ." She blew her nose loudly into her handker- chief. "Oh, God damn it anyway!" So she was crying, after all.

Devlin offered her his handkerchief, waited while she dried her face. "If you have any feelings for me," he said, "you must know that I cannot possibly return them."

"I have no expectations," she conceded. "But it's one thing for me to be seen about London with Violet, and quite another for the Chief Commissioner's daughter to be perceived as one half of a Boston marriage. As much as I might feign disinterest in the mores of society, Inspector, I am not that strongly cast." She glanced at him. "People talk."

Devlin sighed. He'd been doing a lot of that lately. "So your blackmail of me is . . . what, exactly? An attempt to gain respectability?"

"I know what I'm doing." She pretended boldness: doubtless her bravado came from the pages of some yellow-backed novel, where the heroines smoked cigarettes in public places and were bohemian.

"Of course, you do." The entire exchange made him feel sad and quite hollow inside. "Well, you have the advantage, Miss Alcock. I see I shall have to capitulate to your wishes." Perhaps Freddie might be compelled to stand up for him; he'd enjoy seeing Freddie got up in a morning coat.

"Then we have an agreement." Phoebe opened her reticule and extracted a folded slip of paper. "For that, you shall receive a reward, Inspector: one of your letters. You see, I am a reasonable woman."

Devlin didn't even look at it, merely tucked it away in an inside pocket. "Thank you." He walked away from her without a word or a backward glance.

By the time Devlin returned to the Yard, it was nearly two o'clock. He took the lift upstairs and slipped into his office quietly, closing the door behind him. He slumped behind his desk and peered into the depths of his empty, sticky teacup. Marry Phoebe Alcock? He could marry her, if it came to that, if it became necessary. He might have no other choice.

A sharp rap sounded on the door. "Come in." Devlin looked up to see Henry Doyle, Pence's replacement. While he was hardly Pence's equal, Doyle plied his microscope with the kind of single-minded devotion that other men gave to their meals or their mistresses. And while Devlin's colleagues regarded his interest in crime scene samples as egregious, Doyle, like the late-lamented Nigel Pence, thought the inspector was on to something. Ahead of his time, like.

"I had a look at your samples, Sir." Doyle dropped a sheet of paper on the desk. "Afraid there's no joy, Inspector."

Devlin glanced over the paper. "What was it?"

"As far as I can tell, hair ointment."

"Hair ointment. Containing ambergris?"

"'Fraid not, Sir."

So that was that: no ambergris, therefore no readily apparent link. "Thank you, Doyle."

"Sorry, Sir." Doyle slipped quietly away.

Devlin laid his head in his hands. Where was this investigation going? Quite apart from the closet full of empty bottles and the sleeve links, the trail was cold. What did he have to show for his efforts? A human head in a box (now unfortunately missing), a collection of notes all written in differing hands and a dead medical student. "Doyle." He lifted his head. "Doyle!"

"Inspector?"

"Nigel Pence, his personal effects. Has anyone claimed them?"

"No, Sir. We put them aside. We didn't know what else to do with them. Shall I have them sent up?"

"Doyle, you scintillate."

He seemed pleased. "Thank you, Sir. I'll be right back."

Doyle was as good as his word: within twenty minutes Devlin had a cardboard box full of Nigel Pence's worldly goods. He dumped the box out on to his desk: pencils, a spare set of spectacles, one leather glove and a wig.

A blond wig.

The chemist had said that a young man with blond hair had come into the shop to buy cologne; they'd found Pence dead in Whittaker's flat. The description of her tenant that Mrs Higgenbottom had given had been that of a tall man with a burn on the side of his face. Perhaps Whittaker's habit of setting his victims alight had finally caught up with him? Why would Pence be playing errand boy for Whittaker? What was he getting out of it?

"Bloody hell." Pence had been trying to tell him something, that day in the morgue. His speech about the difficulty of finding fresh bodies sounded, in retrospect, a lot like a confession. Whittaker killed them and Pence . . . did what, exactly? Watched? Cheered him on? Bought expensive cologne? If Whittaker was suffering from tertiary syphilis, he'd have all sorts of neurological symptoms to go along with it. Prince Eddy – admittedly the only other syphilitic Devlin knew about – reportedly suffered from a marked tremor of the hands and a general malaise that left him unable to do much of anything. If Whittaker was as sick as Eddy, he'd be in no condition to murder anyone, which meant that Pence must have been acting for him. Probably Pence had gotten carried away (the head in the hatbox? the note in Chimpy's ear?) and Whittaker had lost patience with him. But Pence had been garotted, and strangulation took a lot of physical and emotional strength, which would eliminate a weakened Whittaker.

He went downstairs, nerving himself against the chill of the morgue, and located Pence's body. Perhaps Pence had been poisoned, Devlin speculated, with a substance which mimicked the effects of strangulation, including the protruding tongue and the bulging eyes. He pulled Pence's lower lids down: the eyeballs were cleanly white, with none of the pinpoint hemorrhaging that characterised ligature strangulation. The garotte had seemingly transected Pence's throat, but the extensive bruising that Devlin would have expected wasn't there. He fetched out his magnifier, examined the wound and saw uniformly regular edges of equal depth, as though the throat had been neatly sliced across with a sharp blade. Nigel Pence hadn't died of strangulation. The wound in his throat had been artificially created, after death, and the garotte placed in it at such a depth as to suggest ligature strangulation.

"You canny bastard."

And there was something else, as well: a tattoo on the inside of Nigel Pence's wrist, just two words, but enough to give Devlin a glimmer of hope.

HELL FIRE.

CHAPTER NINE

DEVLIN HAD OFTEN noticed in himself the distressing impulse, when alone, to putter, to dawdle about the premises and tidy things that perhaps did not require tidying, in order that Mrs Taylor not have further cause for complaining about the state of his rooms. He wished he were alone now, that he might putter away to his heart's content, instead of sitting at this dimly lit card table and watching, in mesmerised awe, the motions of the other hands upon the green baize. He'd sat in comparative silence for some time now, watching hands and faces, inhaling the smoke from several expensive Cuban cigars and being summarily prompted now and then by the sharp and none-too-gentlemanly elbow of Reginald Harker. Harker's dubious connections had furnished their entry: some crony of his, another displaced barrister with a taste for worldly vices.

"I see, then, that's five and I'll take another." The man to Devlin's immediate right did some inexplicable thing with the cards, setting the other occupants of the table into subdued motion. Devlin wondered what the devil was occurring, for he had no clue how poker was played, nor had he ever had any inclination to learn. He considered gambling – especially gambling at cards – among the higher forms of vice and wondered often when he had become so stringently moral. At the moment, he was trying to pass for a seasoned card player, with little success. Only Reginald Harker's keen eyes and fine sense of timing prevented Devlin from exposing himself for what he really was. He wondered how fast he'd have to run when these scions of the upper classes figured out he was a copper.

Devlin recognised several important members of high society around the table. He reflected on what Sarah Whittaker had told him, that the influence of the Hell Fire Club reached even into the upper echelons of Society. What would Lord and Lady Saltire think, he mused, if they knew that their red-headed, boyish son was seated opposite Devlin at this very moment, sucking on a cigar (Devlin thought there might be some arcane symbolism in that, but he couldn't discern precisely what it might be) and shuffling cards as if he were a shiftless dock labourer on a Friday night. Their current company comprised that of several snotty ruffians, ne'er-do-wells who floated with ease between the high classes and the low, and who weren't above nicking a spot of crumpet from any of the assorted dollymops that roamed the East End. Devlin had seen their kind before, seen it most profoundly during Saucy Jack's late and unlamented reign of terror. Oh, they'd be quick enough to defend themselves with fancy words and accusations fit enough to drag a man into a duel, but Devlin saw them for what they were and understood their nature.

The club – if it might be called such – was located underground and could only be reached through a complicated series of tunnels and treacherous switchbacks. He'd disembarked from a cab above, accompanied by Harker, and within perhaps ten minutes he was standing in the main meeting hall. It was all mahogany and baize and carpets that seemed to grip your foot about the ankle. Devlin had never actually been a member of a gentlemen's club, not possessing any of the necessary prerequisites for entry, but he knew what he was looking at. This was the place where London's able boys came to rest their weary bones, when the hunt and the horn had lost their savour. He felt remotely nauseous. He was quite nervous, too, in the too-large set of evening clothes he'd borrowed from John Donnelly and the shoes that Harker had bestowed upon him. He'd found what looked to him like fingernails inside one of the pockets but could not determine whether they belonged to Donnelly or Harker, or to one of their resurrected subjects.

The cards were going round the table again, and Devlin felt Harker's elbow in his side, warning him to place his bet. He tried not to fumble the cards, aware of the eyes upon him, the unspoken expectation. "There we are!" He forced a note of cheerfulness into his voice. "I'll raise five."

Again, Harker's elbow in his ribs. Devlin grunted. The men were looking at him, and he saw or felt some frisson of disgust pass between the others. "I say, if you're going to be niggardly, you might as well not play at all." This from a vapid blond man, with the predatory sleekness of an eel.

"From the paucity of your own bet, I should think you'd keep quiet, Ronald." Harker smirked, eyelids at half-mast, and Devlin found himself admiring the silken ease with which the Resurrection Man allayed the unpleasantness of the discourse. "Unless, perhaps, your fortunes are not what they were?"

If nothing else, Devlin had to congratulate Harker on the relative size of his balls, not to mention his slick bravado. "Quite something about the hubbub in the East End," he said. He was aware that he was venturing into dangerous territory, but Reginald Harker was taking a tremendous risk by bringing Devlin in here under false pretences, so it was important to make the most of his visit.

"What about it?" The one called Ronald fleered at him, lips curled in disdain. What was it, Devlin wondered, about the upper classes, that they could so easily achieve that particular expression? Perhaps the projecting teeth . . .

"Well, from what I've heard, this fellow might be the Ripper." Devlin accepted a cigar from Harker, allowed the Resurrection Man to light it for him. The taste was rather stronger than he was used to, and for a moment the table and its occupants swam weirdly before his eyes, but he recovered his composure soon enough.

"So what if he is?" The red-headed son of Lord and Lady Saltire tossed his chips upon the table, the very portrait of elegant aplomb. Devlin suddenly understood why every-body hated the upper classes – even young Saltire had the very same projecting teeth as all the rest. "City needs to be cleaned up. Who cares if he's topping a few old whores?"

"Perhaps so," Devlin allowed, "but what if he's got his cap set for something bigger?"

The blond man snorted. "Like what?"

Devlin shrugged. "Could be anything. You never can tell what might happen." He examined his cards and felt his stomach shrivel in dismay. These buggers were going to take him for everything he had. "I daresay you chaps must know a young friend of mine," he said.

"I daresay we know many friends of yours," Saltire replied. "Everybody wants our company, nowadays." He flickered a glance at another man across the table, a quick look with knives in it. "Who'd you have in mind?"

"Name of Nigel Pence." It was only a hunch, but he'd learned to play his intuition. Sir Neville would have called it "fishing", but Devlin knew enough to keep to whatever worked.

"Word in your ear." The Duke of Bastadge leaned over. "We never use our names here. Just in case."

A clock ticked in the silence, each stroke sounding like attenuated hammer blows. Devlin felt the keen tickle of sweat behind each ear, and his overwrought nerves were twanging savagely.

"Nothing going to happen." This from red-headed Saltire. "As long as this fellow confines his fun to the great unwashed, he can carry on, as far as I'm concerned."

Devlin felt his insides go very still. The room seemed to retreat from him, to become vague, unreal. He darted a glance at Harker, shuffling cards with the impunity of the intimately favoured. "Deal me out," he said. "Need to find the lavs." It was becoming a pattern with him, he thought, that all his most awkward encounters in life should necessitate a trip to the Seat of Ease. He was no more pleased when he found himself wandering throughout the cavernous interior of the club, turning down numerous blind hallways and coming hard against many dead ends. At one point, he had ascended a short flight of stairs and was making for a closed door located at the terminus of the hallway when certain exclamations of carnal excitement caused him to turn about. He found himself hopelessly lost and had decided to relieve himself upon a nearby plumeria when he discerned that he was being followed.

Devlin crept behind a pillar, slowed his breathing to the point where it would be all but inaudible and waited. The footsteps came nearer, echoing eerily in the stony spaces of the underground cavern. He heard the footsteps pause, could almost visualise the intellectual processes of their owner, when a man's head appeared, and then the rest of him. Devlin leapt to collar his opponent neatly. "That'll be far enough, then!"

"I beg your pardon, Sir! How dare you!" He struggled fitfully against Devlin's steely grip, his eyes darting wildly in his head, his lips drawn back over his projecting teeth (there it was again, Devlin thought) like a stallion scenting a mare.

"You were following me!" Devlin pressed the man against

the pillar and gazed at him spitefully. "What d'you think you're doing, eh? Who are you?"

"Lord Dalyrimple, Sir – unhand me immediately!"

Devlin's fingers released their grip; Lord Dalyrimple tidied his clothing with an air of significant resentment and regarded Devlin narrowly.

"Much better," Dalyrimple sniffed. "You might do better than to roam about the corridors yanking people by their clothing."

Devlin waited.

"Yes, well then. I heard you talking at the poker table. I was seated two tables over, with Lord Rumpley and the Duke of Farthe. You're a bit of an inquisitor, aren't you?"

Devlin wondered how he'd come to be linked with the Spaniards all of a sudden, and that nastiness the Catholics did. "I don't understand."

"Mmmm, no vast surprise there." Dalyrimple raised one aristocratic eyebrow. "Cheapside?"

Devlin felt himself bristling, or perhaps it was Donnelly's purloined suit. "I beg your pardon!"

"You're a Yard man, aren't you?"

Devlin raised his eyebrow, but was unable to effectively mimic Dalyrimple's *sang froid.* "And if I am?"

"Let me guess – Brixton. It would have to be Brixton, really . . . not quite low enough for Cheapside, but dear God, where ever did you get that suit?"

"Keep your hands where I can see them!" Devlin snapped. "Unless you'd like to lose 'em."

"You might want to mind your tongue," Dalyrimple

observed mildly. "Talking in the wrong places. You might miss it when it's gone."

Devlin thanked him for the warning.

"I've seen your kind before." Dalyrimple peered at him. "You know nothing, absolutely nothing. You poke around in things that don't concern you, Sir. Dreadful. Absolutely dreadful. Ought to be a law against it."

Devlin turned away.

"Johnny Whittaker – that's what you were asking about, isn't it?" Dalyrimple's smile was slick and oily, like his hair.

"And?"

"Johnny's got them all at his disposal, ready to carry out his every wish."

"Really."

"Some of us have debts, you know – a little too much money spilt about for comfort's sake. Whittaker has an open purse, and nothing buys loyalty like money." Dalyrimple inclined his head. "I'd stay clear if I were you." He laughed noiselessly. "I'd stay bloody well clear."

* * *

If he managed it just right, he could ease himself on to the floor and then . . .

Freddie Collins stopped, his senses tuned to the approaching footsteps along the hallway. He shoved his legs into his trousers just in time.

"Constable Collins!" Violet Pearson stared at him, outraged. "What in God's name are you doing?"

"You've been very good to me." Freddie treated her to his

most winning smile. "But I'm afraid I can't be away from duty any longer."

"You'll do no such thing!" Violet caught the sleeve of his shirt and somehow got the unfastened cuff twisted round his wrist. "Get out of those things immediately and get into bed!"

"No, you mustn't –" Freddie wrenched the sleeve away, stumbling backwards in his weakened state and landing on the bed. "I simply must get dressed!"

Violet caught the front of his shirt in a violent grip, rather like an escapee from a Bluestocking home for wayward girls. "You cannot leave. I forbid it!"

"Inspector Devlin."

"Inspector Devlin is a grown man."

"Violet – Mrs Pearson – please!" Freddie reclaimed ownership of his shirt and righted himself, panting from the exertion. "Please. Inspector Devlin cannot proceed with this investigation alone."

"Mr Donnelly said you were to take complete bed rest."

"Mr Donnelly is an apothecary!"

Violet, seeing that he was not to be swayed, sighed and gave up the fight. "I'll have your things waiting at the bottom of the stairs." She swept out of the room in a cloud of offended feminine dignity, banging the door shut as she went.

Now was as good a time as any to see what was hidden in the wardrobe. Freddie damned himself for a blackguard, but his natural curiosity would not be quelled. Since his convalescence had begun, there had been an excess of foot traffic in and out of this room and whispered conferences outside the door. The two women seemed quite interested in the wardrobe and some mysterious It that was hidden there. He'd overheard Phoebe ask Violet if she could look at It, but Violet had refused: "You cannot keep doing this, Phoebe darling. It will all end badly, I know." Once, Violet had thought him sleeping and had taken the opportunity to rummage; Freddie had watched through slitted eyes as she rifled through the box, lifting and discarding a great many slips of paper, pieces of card and envelopes. Perhaps it was only a collection of mementoes; his own sister kept such a thing, at home. If so, it must have been the most hotly disputed box of paper in the world, given the way Phoebe and Violet were for ever worrying over it. He owed it to Devlin to find the truth.

He opened the box carefully, with trembling fingers.

It was empty.

CHAPTER TEN

I T WAS, DEVLIN had to admit, rather an unusual parcel to
be landing on his desk at this hour of the morning, but
then nothing shocked him any more, or at least nothing
of this small magnitude. A dead cat – a dead cat in a box –
well, that he could take in stride, having seen at least one or
two dead cats before now. The cat wasn't the problem, the
problem was the note that had come along with the cat: *My
lads should have finished the job.* Of course, it was talking
about the recent assault on Freddie Collins, and this made
Devlin's blood boil and froth like a pot of overheated coffee.

Devlin forced himself to swallow the last mouthful of his
cold coffee and found himself wishing savagely that Freddie
might return. At least then the quality of the refreshments

would improve. He carefully avoided examining his feelings beyond that – it wouldn't do for him to get all sympathetic and maudlin about Freddie. Curious means of getting a message through, Devlin thought, but that was Whittaker's style: as flamboyant as possible.

My lads should have finished the job . . . Yes, too bloody right, Devlin thought, or perhaps my lads ought to finish you. The cat, of course, bothered him, because he was something of an animal fancier, but was the sort of thing that Whittaker had always gone in for. This was entirely Whittaker's style – here Devlin allowed himself a small grimace of remembrance – to hurt, and keep on hurting, that was his belief, both creed and tenet.

When they were both boys at school, it had been the same: Whittaker dictated and Devlin obeyed, at least in most things. He could at least say that he had never gone along with Whittaker's campaigns of torment against other boys, nor would he willingly participate in the kinds of gory experiments that Whittaker enjoyed. No, it was different from that: he was Whittaker's shadow, content to trail behind the older boy and feel protected in his presence. Devlin had never truly belonged at the boarding school, but being with Whittaker had helped to erase some of his awkwardness. Being with Whittaker was a sort of protection: as long as he and Johnny were together, then Devlin felt himself to be legitimate. He had gone far, he realised, to court Whittaker's regard and, having gained it, fought like mad to keep it, lest he fade again into invisibility. But that was then, Devlin thought, and this is now. He now only wanted to track Whittaker down and take him in, and then see him swing for what he'd done.

He laid the note alongside the others and examined them all carefully with his magnifier in hand. It struck Devlin as true that a man could only change his handwriting to a certain degree before his own penmanship gave him away. As easy as it was to alter pressure or change the angle of approach, there would always be that one word or letter, that singular jot or tittle that would point, like indices, back to the person who'd written it. The handwriting in all cases was unremarkable, except for the occasional misplaced capital and an unusually hard pressure. The note that Pence had extracted from Chimpy's ear was written in pencil, but the others had been written in ink; the lines appeared steady, without any errors or blots: *I am Down on whores.* In every case, the initial "I" was significantly larger than the surrounding letters and featured a long lead-in stroke. "Bloody show-off," Devlin murmured. Like Nigel Pence's dodgy tattoo, the handwriting wasn't everything – but it was something.

* * *

Freddie had made his way immediately to the Yard – really, there was no other place for him to go – and enquired after Devlin, to see where he could be of best use. It wasn't that he was eager to be back at work – his body felt like it belonged to someone else, and he'd merely borrowed it for a day or two – but he knew that unless he intervened, Devlin would go after Whittaker all on his own without Freddie to protect him. The very idea made Freddie feel inexpressibly weary. It meant that he would have to go chasing after Devlin, probably following him God-knows-where. Once Devlin got a thing into his head, it was difficult to dissuade him.

"He's not been here?" Freddie leaned on the desk for support and hoped it didn't look this way. The desk sergeant applied himself fastidiously to his book and pretended to look interested in what Freddie was saying. "At all?"

"He was here earlier. He went out of here like the bells of Hell, with a dead cat under his arm." The sergeant sucked on his peppermint with a derisive noise. "Like I said, he weren't asking after you, he said nothing about you. Out that door, dead cat. That's all I know."

Freddie sighed gently, twitching at his moustache with a fingertip. He turned round, retraced his steps and went upstairs to Devlin's office. The door opened on a musty interior and no Devlin. The desk was covered in various bits of paper, and Devlin's empty teacup was glued to one corner by a sugary residue. The window blinds were drawn – Freddie wondered when Devlin had last been in – and Devlin's overshoes stood empty beside the umbrella stand at the door. Freddie sat down in the chair and surveyed the office for a moment: very nice. He'd like to have an office like this someday, although (here he smiled gently to himself) he could never be as good an inspector as his guv'nor. He could try, though, and he would do. He considered himself and Devlin as two of a kind, and that was good enough for him.

There was a clattering on the stairs and Freddie sprang to his feet, immediately busied himself at the filing cabinet and feigned great interest in an ancient article about sailing on the Thames – why on earth did Devlin keep such things? – until he was addressed in dry and docile tones by one of the sergeants from down below.

"Yes?" Freddie turned slowly, taking full advantage of his natural grace (and also the remaining stiffness in his back and shoulders) to present an air of haughty disdain.

But the visitor was no one worth posturing for: Dennis Foster had been with the Force as long as anyone could remember and had never attained a higher rank than his present one of sergeant. It was much bruited about that he was dim in his wits and had only received his position through some outside influence, but Freddie could not be sure what that was. Several of the more waggish constables whispered that Foster was Old Brassie's son, begotten on the wrong side of the blanket, but Freddie couldn't honestly see Sir Neville completing the act of coitus with anyone. He was certain that Phoebe had been deposited with Sir Neville through the agency of fairies.

"Are you lookin' for his nibs?"

Freddie blinked at him.

"Devlin! Are you lookin' for Inspector Devlin?" Foster sighed: why in the name of God did they stick the pretty ones in with the inspectors? Clearly, the lad had not enough brains to blow his nose.

"Oh! Oh yes, I am, yes."

"You'll not find him here. Morris, at the desk, said you were askin' after him."

"At the desk?" Freddie glanced behind him at Devlin's

sticky desk, with its surfeit of papers and its empty tea cup, and wondered what he was supposed to be looking for. "Sorry?"

"Bugger!" The expletive exploded out of Foster with the same force required, in another man, to expel a particularly recalcitrant bowel movement. "Morris is the sergeant at the desk! Were you dropped on your head, or what?"

"Well, I have had a bit of a knocking about," Freddie conceded cheerfully.

"Look, Old Brassie told me to tell you that Devlin is gone after Whittaker. I don't know who Whittaker is, or where he come from, or if his mother's givin' a bit of a knees-up at the Pig and Spout. All I know is that Devlin is gone looking for Whittaker, and he said something about Piccadilly – a gentleman's club." Foster exhaled, letting all the air out of himself, and disappeared down a stairwell, still muttering.

Freddie Collins crossed to Devlin's tiny window and gazed out of it for a moment, enraptured with the view: a brick wall and a pair of nesting pigeons whose effluent had painted the scenery in multicoloured strands of slimy matter. Freddie was the sort of man in whom the intellectual dawn is very slow to break, but whose light is staggering to behold. When the light broke, Freddie jolted away from the window as though he'd been shot at, turned and sailed down the same stairs as the deflated Foster.

Outside on the pavements, he paused to reflect while adjusting his gloves. Devlin had obviously got it into his head that Whittaker could be found and neatly captured by merely his own efforts – a dangerous assumption, Freddie knew, especially given what Whittaker's bludgers had done to him. Of course, this plan of Devlin's – if indeed he had a plan – was completely mad, for how could Devlin know where Whittaker was? Perhaps that's what the dead cat was all about. Freddie could just imagine how cheerfully that parcel had been received.

* * *

Devlin was thinking about the dead cat as he sat screened behind the black sides of a four-wheeler, waiting outside a gentlemen's club in Piccadilly. The October chill had seeped into his bones until he felt deadened, cold and stiff, and still there was no movement in or out of the door. He cursed gently, and without any real feeling, as yet another dubious-looking specimen loitered on the pavement, blocking his view of the doorway, but he could have no real hope that Whittaker would even be here. He was going on gut instinct alone, and a sixth sense that told him Whittaker had been here, might be here again soon. Whittaker was a dangerous killer who must be caught, but it went far beyond that now: Whittaker had dared to strike at someone close to Devlin, and for that offence, if no other, he would swing.

Devlin had, for all intents and purposes, cast aside the trappings of a Yard man. Instead of his habitual dark suit and woollen overcoat, he was wearing a selection of ragged clothes that had been handed off to him by Reginald Harker. "I keep these things for . . . situations," Harker had told him, although Devlin had no idea what that meant, and decided not to ask. It probably had something to do with Harker's passion for grave robbing, and, come to think of it, the clothing did retain a rather fusty odour. It would have to do, because Devlin had no time for niceties. He'd been haunting molly houses and gentlemen's clubs (as well as the dangerous places near the docks) for days now, hoping that Whittaker would come looking for another victim. So far, the killer had been irritatingly cautious about his movements.

Devlin slipped out of the four-wheeler and moved into the shadows, eminently grateful that darkness came early at this time of year. He stuck his gloveless hands into his pockets and adopted a rolling sort of stroll, such as a drunken seaman might display, and ambled his way along the pavement to the club. He braced his back against the wall and slowly slid down it to sit with his ragged coat puddled around his knees; the gin bottle was in his pocket, at the ready, and he pulled it out, took what passed for a long drink, the liquor barely touching his lips. Devlin smiled grimly to himself, wondered where Freddie Collins was and hoped that the young constable was safely resting at the home of Violet Pearson in Kensington.

Two men staggered out, leaning on each other for support, and began to laugh hilariously at some private joke. Devlin rolled on to one hip and regarded them blearily, rubbing a dirty hand across his unshaven face. Strangers, no one he knew, and certainly not Whittaker: Devlin would recall Whittaker's features on his deathbed. "Spare us a drink?" The taller of the two wandered over to Devlin and stood swaying over him for a moment; in the cold October damp, his breath steamed out of his mouth and nose and seemed to condense into the air.

"Piss off," Devlin growled, clutching his bottle closer. In the interests of plausibility, it was the cheapest gin available, bought from a street vendor in Mile End and all but guaranteed to bring on a fit of the screaming blue devils in under an hour. To make a scene now would invariably expose his position, and then any hope of subterfuge would have flown out the metaphorical window.

A gobbet of spit landed between Devlin's feet; the man rejoined his companion without another word. Long moments passed, and in the lengthening shadows, a man brushed past him: elegant, well dressed in evening clothes with hat and stick. The hem of his overcoat brushed one of Devlin's shabby knees, and as he went by, the man said, "Good evening, Phillip."

Devlin sat bolt upright, his gaze burning into the man's retreating back. He couldn't be certain that he had heard aright; perhaps the man had merely said, "Good evening, fellow," or something of that like. Nonetheless, he climbed to his feet and followed, careful to keep a proper distance. He had no desire to be arrested and charged with public harassment of a private individual.

The evening cloak was expensive, judging by the way it draped and fell, and the man's shoes were spotless and polished to a mirror shine, their gleam echoed by the ebony walking stick and the silk top hat. He was walking at a moderate pace and with an almost hypnotic rhythm, but for every third or fourth step the walking stick came down a little harder on the pavement: the man was compensating for some weakness. Devlin had seen it before, most notably in his own father: a stroke late in life had robbed him of movement and sensation and rendered him weaker on the left side of his body.

The man stopped to let a hansom cab go by, and Devlin melted into the side of a building. He fished out the gin bottle and sucked on the end of it, peering at his quarry from under his hat brim. The man made no move to cross the street, but merely stood where he was, his hands hanging at his sides.

"Phillip, this really has got to stop."

Devlin's heart slammed into his throat. He raised his head slowly. "I thought you'd be dead by now." Whittaker looked terrible: pale and drawn, with great hollows under his eyes. One side of his face had been burned, and a surgical repair had been attempted, to no avail. The eyes, however, were the same as Devlin remembered.

"Did you get my letters? I didn't write them, you know." Whittaker smiled, his wasted face contracting into a horrible smirk that reminded Devlin of a grinning skull. "My penmanship leaves much to be desired." He held his gloved hands out, not bothering to conceal the violent tremors that rippled up and down his arms. "No, I had a young friend to help me. He's dead now, too. Just like Elizabeth Hobbs. Do you remember her? She made an excellent first subject for my explorations: a single girl all alone in London, without kin, without anyone who cared whether she lived or died."

All the blood rushed to Devlin's head. "John Whittaker, I arrest you for the willful murder of –"

"Not today," Whittaker said. He turned abruptly and

vanished into the surging crowds that thronged the pavement, everyone eager to be elsewhere. Devlin plunged into
the street and was nearly flattened by a charging omnibus; he
managed to roll out of the way in time to avoid being crushed
and staggered back to the safety of the pavement. John Whittaker was nowhere to be seen.

* * *

Devlin, bathed and shaved, was just sitting down to one
of Mrs Taylor's astonishing meals when the downstairs bell
rang. He cursed quietly and cut into the Yorkshire pudding
with more than his usual alacrity. He was chewing when Mrs
Taylor ushered Freddie Collins in, both of them deferential.
On Collins it seemed natural, but on Mrs Taylor it had an
unfortunate effect, like a tugboat struggling to seem dainty.
Collins stood with his hat brim clenched between his fingers,
but Devlin was in no mood for niceties. He pointed the handle of his knife at the constable: "Sit."

Freddie pulled out a chair hastily and slid into it, hands
clasped in his lap. His hat had rolled under the table, but he
dared not dive down to rescue it. Devlin would probably
murder him while he was down there.

"Sir, I can explain."

"You're out of bed." Devlin glanced up as Mrs Taylor
appeared with a second supper, which she placed in front of
Freddie Collins; her smile hovered somewhere between
matronly and salacious, a combination which made Devlin
acutely uncomfortable.

"Sir, I felt that . . ."

"Out of bed, barely healed, and I bet you've been trailing all over London after me, haven't you?"

"I was trying to find you. Foster said you'd gone."

Devlin snorted as well as he was able through a mouthful of beef. "Foster is a drunken sot who couldn't find his arse with two hands and a gaslight."

"You'd do the same for me, Sir, I know you would. I couldn't let you just walk in there, into God knows what, without anyone to back you up, see." This tumbled out in a rush, followed by a moment of acute silence, during which Freddie delved into his plate with gusto.

"Constable." Devlin laid his fork down and gazed at his subordinate. His stomach knotted itself into a curious, gruff tenderness. The bruises on Freddie's face had faded to dappled yellow and purple, and the swelling had gone down, so that Freddie looked like someone had decided to paint his features in with watercolour and hadn't finished the job. "You're still not recovered. You should be in bed! And besides, I can't have you running after me. It's not your task to take care of me. I'm supposed to do that for myself." He bit down hard on his lip. "How are you feeling?"

Freddie smiled. "Another day in that house with those women and I'd have lost my mind."

Devlin chuckled. "Bit much, aren't they?"

Freddie tilted his head, regarded Devlin quietly. "Is it true that you're going to marry Phoebe Alcock?"

Devlin laid down his fork. "I've not decided." Being married to Phoebe would solve several problems at once. Being married to her would securely lay the ghost of his suppressed inclinations; he could forget all of that and be normal, a regular chap with a wife and a proper home instead of this place.

"Still trying to convince yourself?" Freddie didn't seem foolish, inept or particularly idiotic right then. His gaze bored through Devlin with the precision of a cavalry lance.

"Don't know what you're talking about," Devlin said. His voice was hollow and unconvincing, even to himself. He watched Freddie's hands on the cutlery, deft and sure. It occurred to him, not for the first time, that he didn't know Freddie at all. "Phoebe is . . ."

"I know what Phoebe is," Freddie said quietly. "And so do you."

"Not the point," Devlin whispered miserably.

"Right," Freddie replied, "because she can give you children and I can't."

Devlin pushed his plate away. The food tasted like ashes. "Please don't."

"Of course, you wouldn't just be marrying her," Freddie went on as though he hadn't heard, as though Devlin weren't even in the room. "You'd be marrying that other one, and all. Certainly she'd be around all the time, getting under your feet, cluttering up the place." He focussed on Devlin, twisting slowly in a figurative wind. "Unless that's what you're after," he said. "One of them French things, a menage, or whatever it is."

Devlin stared at him. "Are you quite done?" What the hell was Freddie thinking? "Considering I'm your superior, I'm quite astonished that you feel free to speak to me that way."

Freddie let his knife and fork drop on to his plate with an

audible clang. "I wonder what John Whittaker is doing," he said, and, "I expect I'll get an invitation to the wedding."

"I haven't made her any promises." Devlin got up from the table. It had begun to rain outside, a heavy, lashing rain that beat against the windows and drummed on the roof. "She gave very good reasons."

"I'll bet she did." Freddie followed Devlin into the sitting room; the uneven light threw his facial bruises into strange relief. He leaned against the mantle, warming himself before the fire. "I am curious about one thing, though."

"What?"

"Have you any feeling for me at all? Or have I misread the situation? Only I'm not too bright and might need to have things explained to me." He wasn't being deferential: his posture was deliberately casual, but Devlin saw anger in the bunched readiness of his muscles. This was a side of Freddie he hadn't seen before, this angry stranger.

"I don't know what you want me to say." He glanced at Freddie, then away. His own reflection gazed back at him from the dark window opposite; the firelight picked out strands of grey in his hair.

"Right." Freddie nodded – once, as though this were all the confirmation he needed. "I'll go then." He moved so fast there was scant time to react; he snatched up his hat and coat and bolted from the flat, slamming the door behind him. The noise brought Mrs Taylor up from below.

"What was that?" she asked. "Has he gone, then?"

Devlin stared at his own reflection. "He has."

She slapped the remains of their meal upon a tray. "Waste

of good food," she snapped. "Don't expect tea and toast at bed-time!" She vanished down the stairs in a clatter of crockery.

"I won't," Devlin said. The words echoed strangely in the empty room. "I never do."

* * *

Devlin was early at his desk the next morning, a foul morning with a heavy, drenching mist and a chill in the air that went straight to the bone. He'd barely hung his coat before Barnicott appeared, his red hair somehow managing to stand nearly straight up on his head, giving the impression of mind-shattering fear. Devlin supposed it was the humidity.

"Sir Neville wants to see you, Sir, said it was urgent. He's in his office waiting for you."

Devlin waited till Barnicott had vanished before folding gracefully forward and slamming his forehead into the hard wooden surface of his desk. *Damn, damn and double damn again.* What was it this time? Perhaps Old Brassie had heard about Phoebe's overtures and decided to put his oar in. Devlin had visions of being frog-marched down the aisle of the church, with Old Brassie's hand at his collar and a pha-lanx of constables making sure he didn't try to do a runner. Or perhaps Sir Neville desired Devlin's attendance at anoth-er of his wife's infernal tea dances. Whatever it was, it could not possibly be pleasant.

It wasn't. Sir Neville Alcock had a terrible cold, and that, combined with his effusively running nose, gave him the look of a frustrated Brahma bull in heat. His eyes were red about their rims, deceptively weepy-looking, and his lips were similarly wet. He was in a bad temper, too, barging around his desk, swinging his stomach in front of him and pausing now and then to cough resoundingly and spit a slimy organic substance into his handkerchief. It made Devlin queasy.

"I've been looking for you, Devlin." Sir Neville sank his fleshy bottom into the chair cushions and regarded Devlin as he might a mound of horse turds. "I've been hearing things."

"Things?"

"What's this I hear about you taking a four-wheeler and going after Whittaker yourself – in disguise and plainclothes, no less."

Devlin remarked that, as a detective, he always worked in plainclothes.

"Skulking about the streets like a common thief! Lying in wait for him, although I'm certain you got nothing for your troubles. How the devil do you even know this Whittaker is the killer?"

Devlin explained about the chemist's shop, the sweating landlady and her rooms, and Whittaker's sleeve links. "He killed Nigel Pence, or one of his ruffians did. I'm sure of it."

"He has ruffians? I think this run of damp weather has addled your brains, Inspector. Young Pence was an idiot, just like his father."

"Norris Pence was his father."

"Yes, Norris Pence. Blithering idiot. No bloody wonder he came to a bad end. Breeding will out, I always say."

"With respect, Sir, how well did you know Norris Pence?" The wheels in Devlin's brain began clicking and whirring, rather like overwound clockwork.

"He was the police surgeon, worked downstairs in the morgue. Brilliant mind but he lacked the discipline to use it. We used to bring our findings down to him, any time one of the lads came across something unusual. You must remember him."

"And Norris Pence was killed . . .?"

"Murdered, as far as we could tell. Round about the same time as that Hobbs girl. We never found the fellow. They threw Norris Pence's body in a barrel, filled it up with gin and dropped a match." Sir Neville grunted. "Burned like hell fire, it did."

Of course it had. "It's how they discipline their own," Devlin mused. "This whole business of setting fires." He saw Nigel Pence's tattoo in his mind's eye: HELL FIRE. "I need – we need – to bring Whittaker in before someone else is killed." There was a certain sordid inevitability about it that left him chilled throughout. Or maybe that was the weather.

"I know that!" Sir Neville barked, a noise that degenerated into a coughing fit that lasted several long minutes and whose end product was the unfortunate spitting of still more mucus into his already burgeoning handkerchief. "But I can't have my detectives going off on their own, it's not right. You might get yourself into a pack of trouble, and then the Force is all over the newspapers, being laughed at."

Devlin couldn't imagine anyone in his right mind laughing at Sir Neville – at least not to his face – but he didn't say anything.

"You seem dead set on getting this Whittaker, as if he'd done you some kind of a personal injury. I remember the

Hobbs case as well as you, but I can't for the life of me understand why in the world you're so obsessed."

Here Devlin felt it necessary to defend himself. "Sir, with all due respect –"

"Shut it!"

Devlin obediently shut it.

"I've been hearing talk, Devlin, that you and this Whittaker have some kind of a history, something quite beyond this rubbish you keep telling me about being at school together." Sir Neville peered at him, his blubbery lips quivering. "It's no accident that Freddie Collins was beaten, to my mind."

"I had nothing to do with that, Sir. Constable Collins is a very good friend, I would –"

"What I'm saying to you, Devlin, is this: at all times, a police detective must be above suspicion. He must be circumspect, without a stain on his past. These things come back to haunt a man." Sir Neville grunted, not unlike a pig nosing about for truffles. "I know."

Devlin stared at the toes of his shoes. Now all the old ghosts were returning, descending on him like a murder of crows. He still felt incredible guilt over the attack on Freddie and counted himself at least partly responsible – but he couldn't say anything of this sort to Sir Neville, because he knew that to do so would immediately lay all his proclivities bare. How much easier if a man could be himself, if he were permitted to live as he chose, under the aegis of society.

"You are hereby suspended, with pay, for an indefinite period."

This rendered Devlin as speechless as one of Harker's pur-loined corpses.

"I cannot have you going off on your own because you've got some score to settle with this Whittaker." Sir Neville pro-duced another handkerchief, sneezed voraciously and inspected the nasal effluvium that this action had created. Devlin had been dismissed.

* * *

He was packing up his meagre belongings when Freddie came in, bearing mugs of tea and his assortment of facial bruises, all of which were fading nicely. This did nothing to assuage Devlin's guilt, but Freddie's surprise momentarily overrode him. "What the devil . . . ?"

"Suspended indefinitely," Devlin said.

"Has he gone mad?" Freddie put the mugs down, moved to inspect the contents of the box. "You've took down all your pictures. Where's your fern?"

Devlin laughed humourlessly. "I tossed it out the bloody window." He had enjoyed watching it plummet to the alley-way below and smash into a devastated green smear.

"What are you going to do now?"

"What I've been doing all along – my job." Devlin took his still-wet overcoat from the peg and slipped into it. The damp wool hung heavily from his shoulders like a shroud, nearly dragging him to his knees. He forced himself to stand upright, no matter what it cost him, damn it.

"Are you sure that's a good idea?" Freddie came round the desk, stood in front of him, blocking Devlin's escape. "It's my fault, isn't it? I got beat up by Whittaker's bludgers and now you got to pay for it."

"Constable . . ." Devlin sighed through a sudden sharp pain in his heart. "None of this is your fault."

"I'm going with you."

He would never understand what made him do it: he cupped Freddie's face between his palms, his thumb brushing the younger man's bottom lip. His whole being was suffused with a dangerous tenderness. "You are most certainly not. I won't allow it. You've got a future here, Freddie." So easy, he thought, to give in and let himself take what he wanted, nothing standing in his way except his conscience and the law.

"What about you? Who are you going to get to help you? I know you won't let this alone. You'll be out there after him."

Devlin dropped his arms to his sides. "I haven't thought that far ahead. I might enlist Mr Harker's help, I don't know."

The younger man's face fell. "Mr Harker . . . you'd choose Mr Harker instead of me?"

"Oh, for God's sake, Freddie!" Devlin felt all the tension in his body gather itself into a knot, just behind his solar plexus. "Whittaker almost killed you. What makes you think he won't come back to finish the job?"

"But it's all right if he kills Mr Harker?"

"Oh, for heaven's sake!" Devlin burst out irritably. "I don't lo —" He didn't finish the sentence; there was no need.

Freddie squeezed his shoulder. "Just as well, then. Mr Harker isn't quite your type." He smiled gently. "Be careful."

"Mmm." Devlin took one last look around his office.

"Leave a light burning," he said. "You know where to find me."

* * *

Devlin stepped into a waiting cab just off of Whitehall Terrace. He was at loose ends, his authority stripped away; the only thing for it was to go home and stay there, at least until some alternate course of action suggested itself to him. He'd be damned if he'd sit idle while Whittaker and his cronies mowed down renters for sport: if Whittaker wanted to send a message to Devlin, he would do well to deliver it himself.

Devlin climbed the stairs wearily and let himself into his rooms; he declined Mrs Taylor's offer of tea and filled the bath instead. The strain of this case was telling on him, and his whole body felt as though he'd been the one beaten instead of Freddie. He stripped and left his clothes lying where they fell, padded naked to the tub and slipped in, only just suppressing a groan of appreciation. He'd never understood the allure of the newfangled shower baths and preferred his capacious tub; he could read in it and soak or even sleep, although the latter carried with it the ever-present threat of drowning, a profoundly stupid way to die, in Devlin's opinion. What was a good way to die? Of course he'd considered it – in his line of work, everybody did, even someone as gross and degenerate as Abernathy. It had been Abernathy who'd broached the subject one day, as they sat over a glass of beer at the Criterion Bar. "I'd like to go while I'm having it off with some cracking judy," Abernathy had said. Devlin couldn't imagine Abernathy having it off with any woman, cracking or otherwise.

'I'd rather die in my sleep,' Devlin said. Hardly original, but the truth was, he relished the idea of Mrs Taylor finding his dead body. It would be fair recompense for all the times she'd wakened him out of a sound sleep to tell him something utterly inconsequential about situations that didn't concern him.

He never wanted to die as Elizabeth Hobbs had died. No one deserved a death like that, no matter what they'd done. It haunted him, knowing that he could have prevented it, knowing that he was within arm's reach of her, that he could have caught hold of her sleeve or the hem of her skirts and saved her. It wasn't fear that had kept him rooted in place, but rather contempt, the ugly little secret that he had never told anyone, not even Freddie. Not contempt for Whittaker, but contempt for Elizabeth Hobbs. Some part of Devlin believed she could have saved herself, could have prevented the dismal end of her admittedly dismal life. His childhood minder had been Catherine Eddowes, in the days before she took to the streets; some part of Devlin had never forgiven her. He'd seen her on a street in Brixton some months before the Ripper killed her. She'd come up to him and offered herself, not recognising him; her dress was stained with filth and vomit, and she was stumbling drunk on cheap gin. Most of London believed that Gladstone's quest to raise the living standard of unfortunates was ill-conceived, at best; for a long time Devlin had counted himself among them. He had never pitied whores; he had instead resented them. Catherine

Eddowes could have had a normal life, a respectable life. Perhaps what angered him the most was the blind, criminal waste of it.

The water cooled quickly and he got out, wrapped himself in a voluminous Turkish towel and went through to the sitting room. Mrs Taylor had lit the fire earlier in anticipation of his arrival, so he threw another log on and poured himself a glass of whisky. He ought to go over the details of the case, at least get something down on paper, but his mind was numb and empty. The shadows lengthened while Devlin sat nodding over his whisky.

"Drinking in the dark?" The patient voice might have been coming from inside his own head. "That will never do." A gloved hand reached across in front of Devlin's face and turned up the lamp. "It's best if you stay very still."

Of course. Whittaker was fast; Whittaker would run him down and Whittaker would kill him, without the pesky flicker of remorse that Devlin would doubtless feel in such a situation. He'd never make it out of his rooms alive.

"Where's your blue-eyed boy, then?" Whittaker folded himself into a chair opposite. He had deliberately chosen a seat in the shadows.

"His eyes are brown," Devlin said mildly, and, "What do you want?" Stupid question. He knew what Whittaker wanted.

"I've been watching you." A match flared to life as Whittaker lit a cigarette; the air between them stank of sulphur. "You've kept me on the hop." He removed his hat and laid it on the arm of the chair.

Devlin fought to suppress a frisson of shock: the entire surface of Whittaker's shaved and stubbled scalp was criss-crossed with dozens of tiny scars and dents. His forehead was bisected by a line of stitching, the wound only partially healed; one side of his face was horribly burned, the flesh scarred and puckered. Only dimly did Devlin realise that part of Whittaker's lower jaw was missing.

"You've seen my injuries," Whittaker said. "Are you as repulsed as I am, Phillip?"

"What happened to you?"

"I was always the handsome one. It's what happens after a while. It's been a while. And I kept the doctors busy, picking and tapping with their little instruments." He was fairly jiggling with morbid delight. "You thought I'd gone away, didn't you?"

There was a revolver underneath the seat cushions of Devlin's chair. If he could distract Whittaker, if he could get hold of it . . .

"There's a gun underneath your chair." Whittaker giggled at him. "At least, there used to be." He dangled it in front of him. "I remember all your tricks. You've grown entirely too predictable in your old age, Phillip." He toyed with it, snapping the chamber open and spinning it, snapping it closed again. "My injuries are of a social nature. So is my disease." He touched the scars, lingering on each one. "Did you hear that I had emigrated? I did, you know, to Australia. Horrible place." His smile was a rictus, a desperate contortion of his ruined face. "And they've had me in hospital."

Devlin drew a slow breath. "You escaped."

Whittaker stood up and tossed his cigarette into the fire. "It hardly matters," he said quietly. "However, I do advise you to draw off." He bent close to Devlin, his shattered face filling the whole of Devlin's vision. "I can't guarantee your safety if you keep this up. You're meddling about in things you don't understand, Phillip."

The face withdrew, and Devlin waited, his body tensed for the inevitable. The rain beat against the windows; he could hear himself breathing, feel the muted thunder of his heart. "Get it over with," he said. But there was no reply.

Whittaker had left the door open.

CHAPTER ELEVEN

EVLIN ACCEPTED A glass of brandy from Freddie
and waited while the constable sat down beside
him on the sofa. Did he look as poorly as he felt?
Certainly recent events had already taken their toll. He wondered if he could catch the cold-blooded scoundrel that was
John Whittaker, now that the resources of the Yard were no
longer at his disposal. "I suppose Abernathy will be assigned
to it," Devlin said, gazing into the amber liquid. The glass
felt warm in his hand, as though the brandy still held within
it the fire with which it had been distilled. "He'll make a
bloody mess of it – you see if I'm not right." Sir Neville was
concerned about the public's perception of the Force, so he
would want a quick capture and an even quicker conviction.

"They'll find some poor bugger and fit him up for this, you mark my words."

"How are you?" Freddie spoke softly, leaning towards him. All day he'd been wondering what to say to his guv'nor when he arrived at Devlin's lodgings. He hoped he had the words in him to say what he wanted to say.

"Bloody wonderful, Freddie – what d'you think?" Devlin regretted this almost instantly: it wasn't Freddie's fault that he'd made such a bollocks of everything. "Sorry," he murmured. "I'm not myself."

"Yes, you are." Freddie gazed at him with a peculiar intensity that Devlin found unsettling. "Even if you're not on active duty, you're still yourself." He leaned back, frankly assessing the man in front of him. "You never deviate."

Devlin was astonished that Freddie knew a word like "deviate". "Thank you."

"You know who you are, Phillip. That's a lot more than most men can say."

Devlin felt hot colour rise into his cheeks – it couldn't be a blush, he was far too old for blushing. "You're quite full of flattery tonight, Freddie. And I've noticed a new familiarity in your speech. Maybe you ought to get knocked on the head more often."

Whatever else Devlin had been going to say was lost for all time as Freddie leaned in and kissed him. Devlin struggled with his glass, his body coursing towards his constable with the ferocity of the tide; he reached around Freddie and laid his drink on the floor without disengaging from the kiss. His skin was on fire, his pulse throbbing to the tips of his fingers, these fingers that now roamed unashamedly over the young constable's broad back. Freddie's hands reached round to clasp his backside, pull him hard against the younger man in a possessive gesture. Devlin watched, as from a great distance, as Freddie ripped his shirttails out of his trousers and unbuttoned him completely.

The bed came up to meet him, and he had no idea how he'd got there, only that it was soft and warm, and everything would be all right because Freddie was with him now. He turned his face for Freddie's kiss and felt the heat of his desire, transmitted so ably to him in the skin of another. He opened his arms and felt his bones compressed under Freddie's weight, the delicious press and crush of skin on skin. He couldn't say anything. He didn't know what to say. He never did know, in these situations. So he said nothing at all.

*　*　*

Devlin was lying on his stomach with Freddie Collins beside him, and Freddie was running his fingers up and down the furrow of Devlin's spine, pausing now and then at the curve of his back. It was late afternoon, nearly dark, and Devlin felt absolutely boneless, his skin a container for heat. He turned his head and looked at Freddie, saw the smile that curved the constable's mouth. "Freddie," he said lazily, for this was as much energy as he could muster, "you're making me sleepy."

"Let's go for a walk."

Devlin raised an eyebrow. "A walk," he repeated. The sheets were an erotic ruin, and the quilt was somewhere on the floor. His drawers – well, he hadn't seen his drawers for some hours now.

"I love walking at this time of day."

"Aren't you afraid? After what's happened, I mean." He sighed. Freddie was young, and the young never worried about anything at all. "A short walk."

Freddie moved, quick as a mongoose, and rolled Devlin on to his back, pinned him against the bed. "Then we can come back here again." His hands slid down Devlin's sides, caressing, until the detective hissed through his teeth. He wondered where his rational, logical side had gone, that a mere touch from Freddie could so unhinge his faculties.

* * *

"It's gotten away from me, you know." Devlin breathed in the cold air with something like gratitude.

"What's that?"

"This whole case – Whittaker – everything."

Freddie looked at him queerly. "I don't believe you."

Devlin laughed. "I figured I'd have him in custody by now – long before now, actually. I figured I could collar him quick as a thought."

"He's very slippery, like an eel." Freddie, having uttered this pearl of wisdom, looked appropriately blank, but Devlin knew that blankness was part and parcel of Freddie's habitual expression and was therefore not alarmed by it. They had strolled some distance from Devlin's lodgings, talking companionably, with the sensual comfort of this afternoon's pleasures still warm between them. It did not seem strange to

Devlin that they should walk arm-in-arm, for he perceived other men in similar states, all around them. Besides, it felt good to be in close contact with Freddie: he felt he at least had an ally in the midst of all this sordid business.

At length they wandered into a well-lit public house and, disposing themselves around a table, proceeded to warm themselves before the fire. The place was empty save for a group of men in dark topcoats, conversing earnestly at a corner table.

"I always thought, 'If I catch him, I'll have something to show Old Brassie.'" Devlin took a long draught of his beer and gazed at Freddie over the tabletop. "But now I wonder if I'll ever catch him. He could be anywhere. He came to see me the other night, you know."

"Whittaker? Whittaker came to see you?"

"The very same. Told me to draw off or he couldn't be held responsible for the consequences." Devlin laughed mirthlessly. "Perhaps he'll kill me."

There was a man standing before him, a man who had not been there a moment ago. Freddie felt suddenly both hot and cold at once, wondering if they had been observed and listened to. This man was tall, exceedingly well made and might have been handsome had his face not been so horribly deformed. Freddie had seen some photographic prints once, taken on the syphilis wards of some great American hospital, and it struck him that this man, this poor wretch, looked like the men in those pictures. More than that, he looked like the man who'd accosted Freddie in the archives room.

"Hello, Phillip."

202 • J. S. COOK

Devlin froze inside, raised his head slowly, and he and
Whittaker locked glances like two strange tomcats meeting
in an alleyway. He felt the tiny hairs on the back of his neck
come up. He reached into his pocket for the darbies that were
no longer there. Whittaker turned as quick as lightning and
vanished, the door banging shut behind him. Devlin stood so
quickly that he nearly overturned the table, and the landlord
of the place came scuttling over, brandishing a slop pail and
a filthy rag.

"Freddie, stay here." Devlin tossed some coins upon the
table and headed for the entrance.

The autumn darkness had fallen as quickly as ever, com-
pounded now by a dense, thick fog and the rising damps
from the Thames. Devlin squinted, peering into the night,
listening carefully for any sign that would show the direction:
footsteps, the tapping of a stick on the pavement, a cough or
a rustle of clothing.

Nothing.

He slipped one hand into his pocket and went carefully
round the side of the building, where it abutted with another of its like and formed a sheltered passageway, dark and narrow. "Whittaker!" His voice fell damply around his ears,
deadened by the fog. "Give it up and come out."

"Phillip?" Freddie Collins stood framed between the
buildings, peering at Devlin as if his guv'nor had just materialised out of the mists. "What're you doing in there?"

The men in dark topcoats pushed past Freddie Collins to
swarm all over Devlin like a monstrous and demonic horde.
The hand that had been in his pocket came out again,

brandishing a knife as sharp as a surgeon's lance and with a retractable blade, it was his favourite weapon.

Freddie was roaring, laying about him with a certain dogged willingness; Devlin saw nothing except the flashing of his own blade, heard nothing except grunts and swearing all around him. One of the attackers – huge, dark, monstrous – came at him, waving his enormous fists like cudgels, and Devlin drove the blade hard into his solar plexus, dropping him like a slaughtered bull. Another appeared, brandishing a length of pipe and screaming like a berserker. He was stopped – quite suddenly, and probably for good – by Freddie's stunning blow to the back of his head. Of course, Devlin thought, panting furiously from the unaccustomed exertion, Freddie had retained his constable's truncheon and was using it now to good effect.

As quickly as it had begun, it stopped. Their attackers scattered, disappearing into the darkness. The one that Devlin had stabbed lay very still beside the one whose head Freddie had so obligingly bashed in; Devlin had no doubt that they both were dead. He pocketed his knife with shaking hands and tried to mop his forehead with his handkerchief.

"You've done for him." Freddie appeared and turned the dead man over. "He's dead." He laid two fingers against the man's neck and shook his head.

This was bad – this was very, very bad. There would be an investigation, Devlin knew, particularly if their assailants had been, as he suspected, Whittaker's friends and members of the Hell Fire Club. The Yard couldn't possibly turn a blind eye, especially if Devlin had just murdered two "respectable" citizens. He sat down heavily, suddenly very sick to his stomach. The warm feelings of satisfaction and contentment vanished, leaving a howling emptiness inside. Devlin turned his head and retched quietly, each spasm seeming to tear something out of him.

"We have got to go." Freddie crouched on his heels and spoke quietly, urgently. "We can't stay here. They'll waste no time in alerting the Force." He helped Devlin to his feet. "Come on, we have to go."

"Where?" Devlin struggled against Freddie, then subsided and allowed himself to be led away. "Where can we go that's safe? Whittaker must have been watching my rooms. How the devil can he know so much?"

"Obviously these buggers weren't the only ones interested in doing him a favour," Freddie said. "No bloody wonder he's got the run of London. He's got the upper classes in his pocket."

"I don't understand it," Devlin said. "If Whittaker's father disinherited him, where's the money coming from?"

Freddie shrugged. "Maybe he's been calling in some favours?"

"Could be."

"We have to get out of here." Freddie tugged at his sleeve. "Come on."

Devlin dimly perceived Freddie hailing a cab that had stood at the corner; everything was beginning to blur around its edges, and the city seemed strange to him, as if he'd not seen it before. He glanced up at the driver as he got into the cab, his mind remarking that the driver seemed familiar, but perhaps that was only Devlin's addled mind. He didn't know any cabbies personally – he hardly ever used the things, not if he could walk. But the cab was taking an unfamiliar route, and when Devlin darted a glance at Freddie, he saw that the younger man was slouching in his seat and gazing before him with an air of wariness and wily calculation that Devlin had never seen before. "Freddie?"

"It's for your own good."

Devlin moved, intending to leap from the cab, and was quickly restrained by hands that felt so very hard and pitiless, the same hands that had caressed him only hours before. The horrible realisation clanged inside his skull like the tolling of a bell, and he watched in helpless horror as the darkened city slid quickly past them, taking him away.

CHAPTER TWELVE

THE CAB RIDE eventually gave way to a train station – a station that wasn't within the boundaries of London proper, and which Devlin did not recognise. He wondered what Freddie was playing at, and if he, too, was in the pay of Whittaker. It would be so easy, Devlin realised, for Whittaker to corrupt someone like Freddie, someone so innocent and untouched. Almost as soon as he'd had this thought, he dismissed it. Perhaps Freddie had only been toying with him all this time and wasn't as innocent as Devlin had supposed. His demeanour during the long cab ride had been strange, to say the least, for he was more than a little silent and morose, the complete opposite of the young man with whom Devlin had shared a bed earlier that day. Devlin thought dully that Freddie perhaps intended to hand him over to Whittaker, and he wondered why he wasn't trying harder to escape. He merely felt tired, and his hand ached where he had driven it and his blade into the bowels of Whittaker's henchman. He was thirsty and immeasurably weary, and he wanted nothing more than to sleep and never wake again. He could make no sense of anything: Whittaker, Nigel Pence, Phoebe's blackmail, the burned hair of Whittaker's victims and the horrible cologne. Nothing made any sense, least of all this. Why was Freddie behaving so oddly?

Devlin looked about him, measuring the ache in his body against the possibility of escape. The railway platform was deserted, and Devlin wondered if he might make it through to the other side and then on to the tracks before Freddie caught up with him. The cabbie pulled his vehicle close against the station and got down from his perch behind; he paused to tie the reins, and patted the horse's neck amiably, murmuring some comforting phrase meant only for animal ears. Devlin was cold, shivering in the dampness, and his throat felt as though he'd been screaming for a month: sore and gritty and entirely too warm. The station was blurred and strange, as the passing streets had been, and he found himself looking for individual particles of moisture in the fog.

"This way." Freddie took his arm in an iron grip and propelled him into the station, while the cabbie followed, tall and dark and silent as a monolith, carrying a Gladstone bag. Devlin had the odd idea that there was no actual man inside the cabbie's clothes, only a block of stone that had somehow become animated and rumbled after them like a colossus.

This seemed so funny to him that he began to laugh. He laughed until tears ran freely down his cheeks, while Freddie and the cabbie took his elbows and, between them, propelled him on to the train and into a private, first-class compartment that had obviously been reserved for this purpose.

"Here." The cabbie handed a thick woollen blanket to Freddie, whose face had assumed its normal expression of dim-witted vivacity. "Get this around him. He's chilled to the bone, poor thing."

Devlin found Freddie's face very close to his own, and he stared, fascinated. Freddie's bottom lip was trembling, and Devlin noticed that the constable was shivering as badly as himself. Why had the cabbie not given Freddie a blanket? And why had the cabbie left his cab behind them at the station? "Your cab."

"Gently, Phillip." Freddie pressed him back against the seat, his features shuttered by some expression that Devlin didn't recognise. The train lurched forward, forcing itself through the fog as the cabbie pulled down the privacy blinds, enclosing them completely. Freddie reached into the Gladstone bag, brought out a flask and handed it to Devlin. "Have a little drink. It will help you get warm."

Across from them, the cabbie was doing some peculiar business with his face. Strictly speaking, he was peeling off various features and placing them into his pockets, as if skinning himself. Devlin stared at him, wondering if this was some trick of the light, but at last the cabbie finished, rubbed a handkerchief over his face and emerged as Reginald Harker.

"So you're in it, too," Devlin said bitterly. He wanted to

turn his face to the window and weep – with weariness, with regret – but he would remain steadfast. He would go out of life like a man, not sniveling on his knees like a baby.

"I checked all up and down." Devlin realised with a start that Donnelly was seated in a corner of the compartment, holding a revolver. "Nothing much. Two women travelling together and a nurse with a child near the back." The apothecary nodded to Devlin and sat down beside Harker. "Did you see anyone?"

The solicitor shook his head. "No – all the usual precautions – I made sure of it."

Donnelly moved to the opposite side of the compartment, took a seat beside Devlin and pocketed his revolver. "You've cocked that," Devlin said dryly. "I hope you don't shoot your bollocks off."

Donnelly gently touched his face and peered into his eyes. His fingers pulled down the lower lids, raised the upper and then palpated the glands in Devlin's neck. "Not influenza, thank God," he said. "Probably a bad cold. Few days bed rest should help."

"Get your hands off me!" Devlin pushed at him, but all his strength seemed to have drained away. He wanted to lie down and sleep, but his throat hurt and his eyelids were burning hot. He coughed, discharging a globule of mucus that would have made Old Brassie proud, except that it splattered on the floor, somewhere near Harker's feet. The solicitor regarded this with a raised eyebrow, but said nothing. Donnelly reached into a pocket and extracted first a length of string, then a pencil, and what looked to Devlin like part of a finger, neatly severed at the joint. At last he produced a thermometer, which he pushed into Devlin's mouth. The instrument tasted like pocket lint, tobacco and rotting flesh.

Freddie was asleep, his head lolling on to Harker's shoulder. "What's he got to do with it?" Devlin asked, speaking with difficulty around the thermometer.

Harker glanced at the blond head, smiled gently. "He is your greatest ally, Devlin, and perhaps your dearest friend."

"Friend!" Devlin sputtered, nearly choking on the thermometer.

"Sh." Donnelly repositioned the instrument, gestured at his watch. "Just a little while longer."

"Freddie Collins probably saved your life." Harker leaned forward, forearms resting on his knees, his hands dangling. This position caused Freddie's head to drop forward, so that he appeared to be looking for some lost item between Harker's buttocks. "You were quite correct, Devlin. Whittaker has been watching you for some time now. Indeed, I have been following my own line of investigation, and I have determined that John Whittaker has kept you under close scrutiny these many weeks." Harker paused as Freddie awoke and righted himself, smiling idiotically. "He saw you go out this afternoon with Constable Collins. Doubtless he followed you along whatever route your walk accomplished and lay in wait for you."

Devlin glanced at Freddie. "You knew this?" He spat out the thermometer.

Freddie had the good grace to look ashamed of himself. "Mr Harker came to see me whilst I was convalescing in

Kensington. He said we'd to be careful about Whittaker, make sure he kept away from you."

"But at the same time, I had Constable Collins contact Whittaker, without your knowledge, of course, because that would have jeopardised my entire plan."

"Of course," Devlin said sourly.

"Mr Harker said for me to get in touch with Whittaker. I'd some trouble finding him. But Mr Harker managed to get an address, and I've been sending messages, telegrams, like."

"I instructed Freddie to make overtures to Whittaker, offer tidbits of information on your whereabouts and the progress of your investigation." Harker smirked as Devlin's face turned an alarming shade of purple. "False information, Inspector Devlin, you need not concern yourself on that point. False, but with enough truth that Whittaker would think it worth his while."

Freddie was positively preening now. "We knew that he was following you, all along. We encouraged him to do so, in our own way."

"So as to control him, Inspector, control and hopefully contain him." Harker sat back, seeming to lose himself in contemplation of the window shade. "I only regret that your efforts in this case led to your dismissal, but perhaps it's better this way."

Devlin coughed, but into his handkerchief this time. "What d'you mean?"

"We are luring Whittaker away from London." Harker pierced him with a keen glance. "Luring him out into the open, like a wild animal, so that we may hunt more freely."

The solicitor laughed mirthlessly. "One is so confined by the city."

"You're mad." Devlin glanced from Harker to Donnelly – Freddie was looking out the window – and back again. "Do you think he can be so easily led?"

"Oh yes," Harker said quietly. "For he is, at this moment, on this very train."

"He was expecting us at the pub," Freddie said. "I'd struck a bargain with him. I was supposed to lead you to the pub and turn you over to his bludgers."

"But Whittaker had no reason to trust you or Mr Harker, and besides, he probably couldn't resist having a look-in for himself. That's why he showed up at our table."

"I hadn't counted on that," Freddie mused.

"Right." Devlin ground his teeth together. "So if Whittaker had taken out a revolver and shot me in the pub, you'd have done what, exactly?"

Freddie looked blank.

"Oh for God's sake!" Devlin glared at Harker. "I am still a police inspector, Mr Harker. I should like to have been informed."

"Strictly speaking, you are on temporary suspension from the Force, are you not?" Harker's voice seemed to issue from somewhere in his boots. "In which case, you are no longer an official agent." He waved one hand about in front of him. "I merely did as I thought best."

"I'll take comfort in that," Devlin said, "when Whittaker finds me alone and kills me."

* * *

Devlin wasn't precisely sure where they were, except that Harker had taken him to the country, some miles outside of London, and lodged all four of them at a house on the borders of Surrey.

Freddie and Devlin shared a room, as did Harker and Donnelly, but Devlin was by now so ill he could hardly sustain a conversation. He sat on the bed while Freddie filled the bathtub in the other room – thank God for modern conveniences, Devlin thought – and then obediently got in. The hot water quickly lulled him into a state of insensibility, and before he knew better, he was lying in bed, dressed in a clean nightshirt, with Freddie by his side.

Despite his illness, Devlin found that sleep eluded him, and his mind chased itself round and round in circles, seeking answers where there were none to be found. He lay still, listening to Freddie's sleeping breath beside him and the sound of Harker's and Donnelly's voices from the room next door, murmuring in quiet conversation. He watched the shadows lengthen through the curtains and the rise of moonlight that blanketed the bed. He drifted into uneasy dreams, seeing John Whittaker in every corner of the room, and jolted back into wakefulness, his heart pounding and sweat seeping into the sheets. At length he fell asleep, and dreamed that a madman was on a great wooden sailing ship, chasing him and Freddie around below decks with a cat-o'-nine-tails. The ship changed course and sailed off the edge of the world, and Devlin tried to shout a warning, but he could only utter a frustrating series of squeaks and grunts. He tried to cover himself with the sails, to escape the knowledge of the inevitable, but the water rushed in through a hole in the side of the ship, and he had nothing in which to catch it. He woke up shouting and was comforted by Freddie, who fetched him a hot toddy and sent him back to sleep again.

There were no more dreams.

Devlin slept till quite late in the morning, and by the time he finally awoke, Freddie had dressed and gone down to breakfast, and he was alone. He awoke slowly, conscious of the pain in his swollen throat and the hacking cough that racked him. He felt feverish and dizzy, and he sat up slowly, resting for a moment on the side of the bed before attempting to stand.

The day was quite beautiful, one of those cool, crisp days that are only ever possible in autumn, with a sky of soaring blue overhead. Devlin wished he were here in happier circumstances, so that he might enjoy the bounty of the weather. What would it be like to spend a day shooting in this country? He hoped he would have a chance to pursue Whittaker over the entire countryside and lodge a bullet in him, just as he would do with a grouse or a hare. He hoped Whittaker was running away when that happened: Devlin liked the idea of shooting his old nemesis in the back.

As it was, he'd be hard put to navigate the daunting series of meadows and forests surrounding the great house, which stood on a knoll overlooking the countryside. The architecture was of a Georgian style, all columns and rectangles and great big doors. A veritable labyrinth of corridors and narrow, shadowed hallways led away from the main sitting room, and there were several staircases ascending into the upper floors. It was all dreadfully fashionable, Devlin supposed, but he couldn't warm to it. The rooms were terribly draughty, with a persistent chill that even a roaring fire could not dispel; the only redeeming feature was the enormous, well-stocked library with its hundreds of books. Apart from the four of them, no one else appeared to be in residence. Harker had implied that the owners were friends of his, but he'd declined to name them, and Devlin wondered if perhaps Harker hadn't indulged in a bit of breaking and entering. It wasn't beyond Harker's scope.

He looked up as the door opened, and Harker appeared, wearing a sombre expression and an even more sombre dark suit, with lines of fatigue around his eyes and his complexion unnaturally pale. "What the devil?"

The solicitor passed Devlin a telegram, waited while the inspector read it. "Sarah Whittaker hanged herself last night."

Devlin had never considered himself a fanciful man, but now, sequestered with Harker and the others in the country, he began to imagine all sorts of things that would previously have never entered his consciousness. The knowledge that Sarah Whittaker had taken her own life – or had it taken from her – gnawed at his mind. Even given that she was still (as far as Devlin knew) married to John Whittaker, there was nothing in her personality to suggest a tendency towards melancholy. None of it made sense, and he wanted desperately to return to London, to the scene of the supposed suicide, and examine every inch of Sarah's quarters to try and determine the truth. He was doing absolutely no good here, trapped in a bucolic countryside setting with Harker, John Donnelly and a nervous and over-solicitous Freddie Collins hovering at his elbow every five minutes and plying him with tea and scones. Devlin had consumed enough tea in the past twenty-four hours to float an armada, not to mention the increasingly annoying attentions of Donnelly. "It's a sore throat, dammit!" He waved Donnelly and his thermometer away with an irritated gesture. "Just a cold. I probably caught it from Old Brassie the other day."

The papers from London – thoughtfully provided by Harker – brought no fit news for Devlin's ailing state, either. Daily the headlines screamed that there had been another murder, that corpses were found floating in the Thames, lying in the streets, dangling from the chandeliers at the dancing halls. Amazing, Devlin thought sourly, that Whittaker could manage to exact such a monstrous toll on poor benighted London, especially when he was some distance away, but then, the Fleet Street boys were never all that particular about little things like truth and corroborating evidence. Probably some copycat taking advantage of a now wide-open field and an opportunity to get a name for himself. It gave Devlin a kind of grim satisfaction: now that he'd been removed from the case, Old Brassie and all the other high hats in the Force were falling on their collective faces.

"Oh, Inspector, I feel certain that we are on his track now." Harker folded himself into the chair next to Devlin. Today the solicitor was dressed in dark grey, but his strange green eyes held their usual expression of cool self-interest.

"Do you?" Devlin's throat was aching, and his eyelids felt hot and weighted with fever. He'd just been on the verge of drifting off.

"Perhaps it is my intuition." Harker flicked a glance at him, a curious half-smile that appeared and vanished, quick as a thought.

"Well, what the devil are we waiting for, then?" Devlin moved to rise, was stayed by the pressure of Harker's hand.

"All in good time, Inspector." Harker steepled his fingers, assumed a thoughtful air. Devlin found himself increasingly irritated with the solicitor's evasions and wondered whether his initial surmises had been correct. Perhaps Harker had lured him here for reasons of his own. Perhaps he and Donnelly had made arrangements to dissect him, after they'd done away with him, and add their findings to whatever dubious research that Harker was currently involved in.

"I have been examining this Whittaker's movements. He was indeed on the train with us, and he is here, just near by."

Devlin coughed noisily, dislodging what felt like part of his right lung. "Post handbills, then," he hissed, "and tell him to show himself so I can arrest him."

"No need to post handbills, my dear fellow." Harker smiled insinuatingly, clasped his hands around his knees. "He sticks closer than a brother."

"What d'you mean, he's close? Close to what?"

"Close to us."

The walls seemed to bend and bulge curiously, and Devlin passed a hand over his eyes until the fit had passed. He couldn't imagine what Harker meant: even given that the country house was large, Devlin could hardly fail to discern Whittaker's presence in the hallways. "Where?"

"He got off the train at the same stop as we did and took rooms in an inn called the Chequers, about a mile down the road. I have gone there several times, on some pretext or other, and twice now I have sent John."

Devlin was dumbfounded. He knew that Harker liked to play detective, but he hadn't factored this sort of cool subversion into the solicitor's character. "You said he took rooms – not just one room."

"Ah – he is there with his sister."

"His sister?" Devlin didn't remember a sister. If Whittaker had a sister, this was news; if he had a sister who was clearly in collusion with him, then the case before them was considerably enriched. Perhaps it hadn't been Pence who'd written the notes, but Whittaker's sister. "What sister?"

"Violet Pearson is his sister." The words clanged in Devlin's ears like the tolling of a bell.

CHAPTER THIRTEEN

"I'M COMING WITH you," Devlin said. Perhaps he'd die chasing Whittaker, but he'd be damned if Harker was going to run the show. Devlin hadn't wanted to make so bold a move as lying in wait for Whittaker at the Chequers, but he told himself that, since he could find no better method of capture, it was just as well to follow Harker's advice and see what came of it. The worst that could happen was that Whittaker would divine their presence and take himself away, leaving them empty-handed.

Devlin had allowed John Donnelly to bundle him in a heavy overcoat and a knitted muffler, against the late October chill. The fields around the country house were white with frost, and there was a scent of snow in the air. The cold lay upon Devlin's chest like lead, and he coughed uncontrollably in the carriage, raising concerned looks from both Donnelly and Freddie. Harker, for his part, was too sunk in his own reflections to pay much attention to the beleagured police inspector, and Devlin wondered what was going on in Harker's head.

"Are we there yet?" Freddie Collins sat with his buttocks barely touching the edge of the seat, and his gloved hands wrung themselves together. "When are we going to be there?"

Everyone ignored him. The silence inside the carriage grew, punctured only by the sound of the horse's hooves on the road. Someone's stomach growled, and Devlin found himself wishing mightily for a cigarette, but Donnelly had forbidden it, on the condition of Devlin's lungs. Devlin wondered peevishly just when John Donnelly had received his medical certificate. It seemed the apothecary was giving himself unwarranted airs, but Devlin supposed that his dubious medical attention was better than none, especially at a time like this.

Harker had assumed the poise of a predatory animal, sitting pressed against the cold wall of the carriage, gloved hands clasped together in his lap and his eyes hooded and watchful. Devlin still didn't entirely trust him: it wasn't beyond Harker's scope to be somehow involved with Whittaker, especially if there was benefit in it. Devlin imagined that Harker would sacrifice even his acolyte Donnelly if it meant an advance in his own position.

"How do you know he'll be there?" Devlin raised his face from the muffler and directed his question at Harker. "It's not like he's expecting us, is it?"

"Harker thinks he has devised a means by which Whittaker can be made to show himself." Donnelly nodded his agreement, as if he had been the instigator of this great and noble scheme.

"Oh, has he?" Devlin cursed quietly. "What did you do," he asked Harker, "send him a telegram?"

Harker turned his head slowly, his eyes slow to focus, as though he had just then been lost in some unfathomable inner contemplation. "Why yes . . . that's precisely what I did, Inspector."

"You did." Devlin tried to laugh, but incited another coughing fit. "And I suppose you requested the presence of his sister, too?"

"I have laid an amiable trap. Whittaker will step into it because he will be unable to resist."

"And he's just going to overlook the fact that you have lent me your abilities . . . put it down to a brain fever or something?"

But Harker was no longer listening, and after a moment the carriage ground to a halt in front of the Chequers. "We're here."

The interior of the inn was overheated by a blazing fire on the hearth, and, wrapped in his woollen overcoat and Donnelly's great muffler, Devlin began to sweat. He sweated as a pudding sweats when placed into a bag and secreted within the same pot as a boiled dinner. His perspiration ran off the tips of his fingers and into the recesses of his gloves and crawled a slow and agonising pathway down his spine. He glanced around the room, taking careful note of the several quiet patrons disposed around the tables, and spotted John Whittaker, seated near the back. Even deathly ill, Whittaker was beautifully dressed, with an understated elegance that Devlin had always envied. With him sat a woman dressed in gentlemen's attire, smoking a cigar.

Violet Pearson.

Devlin swayed, and clutched at Freddie Collins who, in the interests of verisimilitude, had shaved off his moustache and slicked his curly blond hair back over his head. The effect was not unlike a squeezed ferret being forced headfirst through a length of piping. Freddie was dressed as a gardener-cum-jack of all trades, and someone (probably Harker, knowing his penchant for dressing games) had smudged coal dust on several strategic places around Freddie's face and head. He looked for all the world like a Northern miner just home from the pit and headed for a bit of a knees-up at the local pub. Harker and Donnelly had seated themselves at a table close to where Devlin was hiding: Harker had assured Devlin he would keep a careful eye on Whittaker.

"Quick." Devlin stepped backwards, taking Freddie with him. "He's got astonishing eyesight. I'll be surprised if he hasn't spotted us already." He crouched behind a printed Chinese screen and blinked through the haze of smoking candles. Whittaker was drinking but not eating, despite the full assortment of food on their table. "Does he look worse than when we last saw him?" Devlin whispered.

"It wasn't but a couple days ago that we saw him," Freddie replied, "so it's hard to tell."

Devlin motioned to Harker and withdrew, taking advantage of all available cover until he and Freddie were safely secreted in a back room. This was very bad: he hadn't counted on Violet Pearson, but now that she was here, he could hardly snap his fingers and vanish her away. And while this particular charade was going on they were wasting valuable time, time better spent in capturing Whittaker. "I should go and arrest him right now," Devlin said.

"You can't," Freddie replied. "You've no warrant card, remember? And what if he decides it's worth his while to hurt Violet? Do you want that on your conscience?"

"My conscience hasn't anything to do with this, Constable."

Freddie stiffened. "It's 'Constable' now, is it?"

"Freddie."

"Do you want Violet to be another Elizabeth Hobbs?" Freddie was pale with anger. "Is that what you're after? Because that's what will happen if you go charging out there now. All he's got to do is grab her and put a pistol to her head. You know him. You know bloody well he'd shoot her in front of everybody without a flicker of remorse."

Devlin hated it when Freddie was right. "So it's Violet you're worried about."

"I'm worried about you and all," Freddie replied. "And Mr Harker and Mr Donnelly and everyone." He ducked his head, picking relentlessly at a worn patch on his coat. "And me. I can't get killed just yet. There's things that want doing, and I'm the man to do them."

"You're the man to do them." Devlin opened the door a

crack and peered through the narrow aperture. "You're a flaming idiot."

"Thank you, Sir."

"Smoothly done, Inspector." Harker slipped into the room at great velocity (nearly bowling Devlin over) and closed the door. "I am certain you were not discovered."

Harker flicked a glance at him. "I am satisfied that she is not complicitous in this affair."

"Really." Devlin felt sweat running down inside his pant legs, collecting in his shoes, and he wanted nothing more at that moment than to bash Harker a good one in the mouth. But that would bring Donnelly down on him, and he'd heard that the apothecary had played rugby football at school.

"When do we take him?" Freddie asked.

It irked Devlin that the question had been addressed to Harker instead of him. "What are you talking to him for?"

The door swung open and shut, and Donnelly was in the room. The apothecary was carrying the revolver he'd brought with him on the train. "Violet is all right for the time being." He addressed himself to Harker. "I don't favour putting her in danger, Reg. We should have thought of some other way."

Harker was momentarily shamefaced. "I despise the risks as much as you, John, but truly, there is no other way. The lady herself proposed it, and who am I to refuse her?"

"Wait a moment," Devlin interposed himself between the two men. "What are you planning? What risks?"

"Harker has arranged this meeting. Violet is part of the plan. As Whittaker's sister, she has his confidence, and it's necessary to get Whittaker away from here and into some place more secluded." Donnelly wrestled a breathless Devlin into a chair and loosened his muffler. "If we pounce on him here, the whole thing is finished."

"You're a bloody piece of work!" Devlin spat some woollen threads on to the table and cast the muffler away from him with an expression of distaste. "I suppose you cooked this up between the two of you, eh? Is that it? Cut Devlin out altogether, let Harker ponce on in and take the credit."

Freddie bit into a particularly stubborn hangnail with perhaps more force than was necessary. "What docs that mean," he asked, "ponce?"

Devlin ignored him. "What's he going to do? Lure Whittaker out on to the lawn and beat him with a rake?"

Donnelly caught Devlin's wrist in a powerful grip. The apothecary's brown eyes were cold and uncompromising. "He is going to lure him back to the house."

The tiny hairs on Devlin's forearms stood to sharp attention. He stared at Donnelly, open-mouthed, while Freddie gnawed his fingernails in contented silence. "The house," he said finally.

"This was his intention all along." Donnelly released him, sat back as a waiter appeared, bearing hot drinks for them on a tray. Devlin sniffed the cup, detected an aroma of rum and spices, and wondered if Donnelly and Harker had planned this aspect of it, as well. It certainly wasn't beyond the realm of possibility, given the means by which Harker had lured both Devlin and Whittaker here. Obviously the solicitor had depths that his bloodless exterior had never even hinted at.

"So what are we supposed to do in the meantime?"

"We shall return to the house and wait."

* * *

Harker had nearly worn out the carpet in front of the fire-place, and his ceaseless pacing was making Devlin dizzy. The cavernous sitting room was freezing cold, which did nothing to lighten Devlin's mood. He was quite nauseous, courtesy of his drink at the Chequers, and any moment he felt he might be compelled to hurl the contents of his stomach on to the hearth rug. His fever had reasserted itself, and he felt flushed and peevish; he kept falling into a fitful sleep, only to be awakened by Donnelly's grunts of exclamation. "What are we waiting for?" Devlin asked. His voice sounded thick and choked with mucus, and his skull was pounding rhythmical-ly. "It's obvious he's given you the slip."

Harker whirled around, suddenly furious. "I will not accept that!" he roared. He subsided into silence, assumed a pose before the mantelpiece, one hand upon his hip and the other pressed against his forehead.

The outer door clanged shut, and footsteps sounded in the corridor. Harker lunged, but Devlin was quicker. He yanked the door open.

"I couldn't . . . I couldn't persuade him." Violet Pearson stood there, elegant and beautiful in gentleman's clothes. "I did everything you told me." She glanced at Harker, loung-ing near the fire. "It was as if he knew something. I couldn't make him come here. I'm sorry."

Freddie took her arm, drew her near the fire and poured

a glass of brandy for her. "It's not your fault," he said. The firelight played off the dirty smudges on his face.

"This throws difficulty into the whole arrangement," Harker sniffed. "Now I shall have to start all over again."

"No." Devlin felt the time had come to assert himself. "You'll do nothing of the sort. In the morning, I am going back to London, and I am going to demand that Sir Neville Alcock reinstate me, and then I am going to track Whittaker to his lair and I am going to arrest him." He sounded far more confident than he felt, but at least it was a start. Now to get the case back on track, back within the aegis of the Force, and get some work done.

* * *

Characteristically, Devlin went charging back to London, with Freddie at his side and a supply of fresh handkerchiefs in his pocket. Donnelly and Harker had elected to stay in the country for a few more days, as it was coming on for the weekend, and Harker felt that, as he put it, "a respite from our onerous labours" was in order. Devlin had never in his life seen Harker perform anything like onerous labour, but he wisely held his tongue. Donnelly had given him a supply of the same viscous substance he had previously poured down Devlin's throat, but Devlin tossed it out the window of the train as soon as they pulled away from the station.

"You could have stayed, spent some time in the country, enjoyed yourself." Devlin peered at Freddie. The young constable had been curiously quiet all morning, and Devlin wondered what was bothering him. "I'm sure Harker wouldn't have minded."

"I should be with you, Sir . . . Phillip. And I'm still on duty." Freddie gazed out the window at the passing country-side. "I had to send a telegram saying I was sick. Old Brassie doesn't know I came away with you. He thinks you're at home with your feet up."

For the first time Devlin realised the depth of the sacri-fice that Freddie had made, the depth of all the sacrifices that the constable had been making ever since this sordid business began. He felt acutely ashamed of himself, that he had never thought to offer one word of gratitude. Surely the constable deserved better. "Thank you." It felt awkward, and Devlin wasn't sure he could get the words out his mouth, or perhaps it was Donnelly's vile muffler. "You've been . . ." He sighed, huffed his breath out between his teeth. "See here, Freddie, I mean, you've been absolutely top hole about this, right from the start." He stole a glance at Freddie: the constable's cheeks were flushed with pleasure. "I feel badly that I've put you in such danger." It was true: ever since Freddie had been set upon by Whittaker's bludgers, Devlin had impressed upon himself how vital it was that Freddie stay out of the line of fire, that Freddie was his subordinate while he, Devlin, was the man in charge. Had been the man in charge, anyway, until Old Brassie gave him the heave-ho.

"I'd go anywhere with you." Freddie raised his head. "You know that. I'd cut off my right arm if you had want of it."

"You're left-handed," Devlin observed. "It would hardly be such an entire handicap." He smiled. "You're a good 'un,

Freddie." The effect of all this affection was making him slightly nauseous; it wasn't like Devlin to say the things that he was feeling, even if the situation seemed to demand it. He had always believed that actions spoke much more forcefully than words, but he thought that perhaps others might like to hear him cast about a few platitudes now and then.

"What do you think he's going to say?" Freddie fished out a handkerchief and dabbed at his eyes. "Dust," he explained, when he saw Devlin looking.

"Old Brassie?" Devlin permitted himself a humourless chuckle. "He'll probably clap me in irons, or he would do, if he could."

"We've got nothing though, have we? Some notes that could have been written by anybody."

"Some notes that were all written by the same person," Devlin amended. "Handwriting is extremely difficult to disguise, try as you might. There's always some common characteristic. Doyle said that Pence never wrote at work, so the handwriting he showed me wasn't even his. The fact that we found him dead in Whittaker's rooms is a definite link between the two of them." He allowed himself a short laugh. "No wonder Pence was so enthusiastic about Chimpy Darwin's head. He was for ever going on about the shortage of good cadavers, how hard it was to get hold of fresh bodies."

"You should have sent him to Mr Harker," Freddie chided.

"If Pence was as desperate as he claimed to be, he'd probably be more than willing to help Whittaker out by killing for him, one Hell Fire member to another. It would give him an endless supply of fresh bodies. Who knows what Pence's relationship to Whittaker was? I'm absolutely certain of one thing, though."

Freddie was silent.

Devlin sighed. "You're supposed to ask what I'm certain of."

"Whittaker murdered Pence," Freddie said. "That's why the garrotte was laid in the wound, to make it look like he'd been strangled, when all the other victims had had their throats cut." He blushed. "Sorry, Sir. Did I steal your thunder?"

"Bit late to be apologising," Devlin sniffed. "Perhaps Pence was meant as a diversion: Whittaker thought that if he made it look like Pence had been strangled, we'd suspect a second killer. Of course it's far more likely that Whittaker killed Pence himself."

"No honour among thieves," Freddie said.

"Or murderers." Devlin sneezed several times in succession, blew his nose loudly in his handkerchief. "This illness is a damned inconvenience," he said.

"So Pence and Whittaker struck a bargain, and Pence got free cadavers."

Devlin was amused. "You sound confused, Constable."

"Why Pence, though? He could have hired any medical student at all. They're all desperate for fresh corpses," Freddie remarked. "Why go to the trouble and bother of contracting Pence?"

"Because Pence was on the inside," Devlin replied. "With Pence in place at the Yard, Whittaker had a constant source, an extra set of eyes for ever feeding him information."

Freddie grimaced. "Bit of a disgusting image, Sir."

"Sorry." Devlin chuckled. "Whittaker's notes were direct quotes from Jack the Ripper: 'I am Down on whores' and so forth. If Elizabeth Hobbs had infected him with syphilis, wouldn't he kill prostitutes?"

"I give up," Freddie said.

"I'd be willing to lay good money that Whittaker was never near Elizabeth Hobbs. He probably contracted syphilis from some down-at-heel renter."

"So killing male prostitutes is the perfect way to revenge himself." Freddie sat back in his seat. "That's a bit . . ."

"Mad." Devlin patted Freddie's arm. "It's a bit mad. But it's predictable. Murderers are always predictable, sometimes in unpredictable ways."

"Yes, but . . ."

"But what?"

"Why kill Elizabeth Hobbs in the first place?"

"Because she'd come to me for help." Devlin felt the sting of tears at the back of his eyes. "She'd come to see me, said a man was following her, harassing her. I promised to help her. And Whittaker's man on the inside relayed the information."

"Right, you've lost me," Freddie said. "How the flaming heck did Nigel Pence manage to get a job in the morgue when he'd have been . . ." Freddie counted laboriously on his fingers. "Young."

"Nigel Pence was still at school. Ten years ago, the police surgeon was Norris Pence."

Freddie stared at him. "His father."

"I did some research on the Hell Fire Club," Devlin said.

"When Mr Harker and I spoke to Sarah Whittaker, she said that fathers often initiated their sons into the club. I found a tattoo on Nigel Pence's body."

"Hell Fire," Freddie said. "I remember reading about it." He hastened to explain. "Distant cousin on my mother's side had been a member – years ago, before I was born. It's horrendous."

"The tattoo?"

"Any of it, Sir. They dare each other to do horrible things." He fell silent. "I don't think I'd ever have it in me to hurt anyone for fun."

Devlin smiled at him. "Cheer up, Freddie. You made it into our club. We have a lot more fun."

"Yes, Sir."

* * *

Sir Neville Alcock didn't necessarily need to clap Devlin in irons: as soon as the train pulled in to St Pancras, Devlin understood the true length and breadth of his difficulties. "See this?" Freddie came towards him, bearing a newspaper. "They're making a bleeding show of you!"

"Bugger." Devlin caught Freddie's arm and pulled them both back against the wall. "Let me see that." He coughed into his handkerchief till black spots swam before his eyes. His nose was running like a leaky laundry tub, and he felt generally chilly and unwell. He wanted nothing more than to crawl into bed and stay there for at least a month.

"Not good news I'm afraid, Sir." Freddie handed him the newspaper.

Oh yes, there it all was, in plain black for all to see: Inspector Phillip Devlin, lately of Her Majesty's Metropolitan Police Force, wanted on the charge of murder, two young gentlemen (Devlin snorted) found gravely injured in a laneway during a fracas, assistance of the public requested in apprehending this dangerous madman. Devlin tossed the newspaper away from him and tried to think. The morning sunlight was streaming past the rising mist, casting long shadows on the platform, lighting up the window glass and the brass door fittings and glistening in Freddie's blond hair. Devlin envisioned his future as a series of doors, all shut upon him, leaving him in blackness and privation.

"What are you going to do?"

Freddie's voice snapped him back to reality. "You go back to work, Freddie."

"Yes, but what are you going to do?"

Bloody good question, Devlin thought, considering the pickle he was in at the moment. "I'm going back to Surrey."

Freddie's eyes widened to at least twice their normal diameter. For some moments his mouth worked soundlessly. "You're going back to Surrey. Alone, on the train, with no one to see to you and that maniac waiting for you?"

"Freddie, I'm a wanted man. If this gets processed through the courts, I'll swing for it. Mr Harker and Mr Donnelly are in Surrey." Devlin had witnessed many a hanging in his time; he wondered grimly if he would now witness his own. "I'd prefer to apprehend John Whittaker on my own recognisance, but I can't risk approaching Old Brassie. This is how it has to be."

His arm was caught and held. "I'm going with you. Wherever you're going, I'm going too."

Devlin sighed. "I appreciate your loyalty, Freddie, but right now isn't the time."

"It's got nothing to do with loyalty!" Freddie hissed. "Good God, man. In spite of my own better judgement, I care what happens to you. And I know you and Mr Harker and the rest all think I'm as thick as pudding, but I can help."

This was getting him nowhere. It was all fine and good to argue with Freddie, but to argue with him in the broad light of day in St Pancras station was quite another, especially as things stood now.

"All right," he said wearily. "You win." He was obscurely grateful for Freddie's persistence, thick-headed though it might be. "If Whittaker kept a man on the inside, then so can I. You said there were things that needed to be done, and you're right, you are the man to do them. If you do this for me, well . . . I'd be grateful."

"Tell me what you need."

He dispatched his instructions quickly, waited till Freddie had gone, and then boarded the train back to Surrey and Mr Reginald Harker.

CHAPTER FOURTEEN

DEVLIN WAS JUST unlucky enough to catch Harker and Donnelly in *media res* or *ad hoc* or whatever that Latin phrase was. Devlin hadn't got much Latin at school, despite the best efforts of his praeceptors . . . in *flagrante delicto*, that sounded about right. "Inspector!" Harker started up with a force of strength that Devlin would have hardly credited; his intensive search for various items of his clothing was also impressively energetic. "We had no idea."

Devlin felt an odd satisfaction at the blush on Harker's thin cheeks, but he suspected that Donnelly was rather less than thrilled at his sudden reappearance. "I'll just wait in the sitting room, shall I? Until you both have . . . er . . . composed yourselves." He followed the winding series of passageways back to the front of the house and helped himself liberally to the sherry while he waited for the Resurrection Men.

"Mr Harker didn't say you'd come back."

Devlin started violently, cursed himself for being so sunk in his own thoughts. "Mrs Pearson?" He laughed bitterly, recognised the entire premise for the savage endgame that it was and resigned himself to whatever might follow after. "Johnny never told me that he had a sister. I suppose it never came up. Not like other things came up. But I guess you know that, and all . . . my history with your brother, the whole sordid bit."

"I'm not intending on blackmail, Inspector, if that's what you think." She moved to the decanter and poured herself a glass of sherry, drank it off without even blinking. "I want an end to all this, just like you." She went to a cupboard in the corner and opened it, withdrew a small bundle of paper. "I'm afraid Phoebe isn't built for subterfuge," she said. "She did try her best, but was unable to keep a secret. She hasn't any talent for stealth." Unlike you and me, her eyes said. "At any rate, there are your letters, Inspector." She laid the bundle in his hands.

He untied the ribbon holding the bundle: all his old love letters to John Whittaker, all of them lovingly preserved. "He didn't keep them," Devlin said. "Your brother said such gestures were weak and foolish."

She smiled, but there was something of sorrow in it. "He lied to you, Inspector. Before John went to Australia, he placed these in my trust. He pressed me to publish them and discredit you."

"When your father died, all his wealth passed to you, did it not?"

"I never believed what my father did was right. He should not have disinherited John. It was a cruel thing to do. But my father was very set in his views, and would not be swayed. He believed that he was doing right. I married well, Inspector, and had no need of my father's money, so I deposited the whole of it into an account in John's name." She lifted her chin. "He is still my brother."

Devlin reached for the decanter and lit a cigarette, John Donnelly be damned. "I've figured out most of it," he said, "but one thing still isn't clear to me . . . even after all this time."

"Yes?"

"What part are you playing in it? I mean, what's your role?" Devlin offered her a cigarette, which she accepted and lit for herself. "I can understand the posture of the doting sister, keeping a hand in with the poor, misunderstood and wayward brother – next you'll tell me it was your mother's deathbed wish or your dead old papa's bequest – but how much did he have to pay you?" Devlin waited. "To do poor Sarah in, I mean."

Perhaps it was his awful, chesty cold, but her hand had smacked into his face and rebounded to her side before Devlin could even think of uttering "Jack Robinson". A warm, stinging flush spread along his cheek, darting pain into the socket of his eye.

But Violet was weeping. "Sarah was my friend!" She scrubbed at her tears angrily, ashamed that Devlin had seen her momentary weakness. "We were at school together . . . we'd made plans with each other, you see. Only Johnny had to put his oar in."

Devlin made no effort to hide his confusion. "What d'you mean?"

"Oh . . . coming round her house of an evening, bringing flowers or chocolate, all the sorts of things that men do. She could hardly refuse him, and I resigned myself to it, because I thought that she'd be well cared for." She cast a defiant look at Devlin. "It's not like you might think, you and Mr Harker and the rest. Sarah and I were like sisters! There was a bond between us." She poured herself another drink and retired to a chair.

"I'm sorry . . . that she died." Devlin let it drop: no sense in digging up old bones. He'd leave grave robbing to the likes of Harker and Donnelly who were now both clothed, after a fashion, and both bearing glasses of brandy. Harker was smiling, but Devlin thought he could detect an undercurrent of hostility in Donnelly's smile. Well, it couldn't be helped, and he'd no time to consider the social niceties when Whittaker was stalking around Surrey with the bit between his teeth.

"Forgive our inattention, Inspector." Harker inserted himself into a chair, folded his limbs into the approximate posture of a preying mantis and treated both Devlin and Violet Pearson to a particularly bloodless smile. "We were . . . engaged."

"I just want this to be over with." Devlin, feeling suddenly old and tired, leaned against the mantelpiece. His reflection gazed back at him implacably: a man of middle age with circles underneath his eyes and two bright spots of fever burning in his cheeks. "As soon as possible. So I can get back to London and clear my name and get on with things. I've no taste for buggering around." Perhaps the wrong choice of words, he reflected, but he'd worry about his social gaffes later on.

"No need for buggery, Inspector, whether metaphorical or otherwise." Harker levelled a gaze at him. "Mrs Pearson has summoned her brother here, to this very house, under false pretences."

"My brother is suffering greatly in his mind, Inspector. If he were truly in his wits, he would want an end to this, I know it."

The front door clanged, the bell perhaps manipulated unduly by the shivering October wind. Harker's head swivelled as though mounted on gimbals, and Devlin saw him exchange a look with Donnelly: secretive, furtive, altogether culpable. "Ah," he said, "I see."

The footsteps entered the front hall and paused just there, in the foyer . . . a sudden, unexpected foray into the kitchen and the butler's pantry, then a shift, a forward impetus, moving irresistibly now, drawn towards them as though fastened by a length of thread.

"Violet? Where are you?"

And he was standing in the doorway, gazing at them with a certain eerie patience. He nodded at Devlin. "I did warn you, Inspector."

"John." The utterance caught Devlin by surprise and rasped itself against the insides of his throat, hurting him.

The room was floating oddly about him, textures of things all wrong, the light was bending, quick and agile, and the beating of his heart was out of rhythm. "John Whittaker."

The monster laughed – a gentle laugh, full of the most horrible loathing. "You shouldn't run about like you have done, Phillip. It weakens the body, so much haste."

Devlin slipped a hand into his pocket, felt about the lining of his coat with icy fingers. It would only take one, he thought, but he could be wrong, because the room was weird and tilting now, and things were sliding past him. The footsteps were back, above his head and all around him, and he could see the danger now, the danger in the revolver held in John Whittaker's gloved hand. He had to watch the hand, watch it move, see the fingers clasp and reach, all of it so horribly slow and there was nothing he could do about it.

The shot rang out, and he was deafened by it, sickened by the stink of cordite and the writhing, slippery motion of the body as it fell face down on the carpet. The blood was coming out and pooling all around the head, and he could see the jagged hole the shot had made – and he could see Violet Pearson in the passageway, her right hand white-knuckled on a revolver, a curl of smoke dying slowly in the stillness of the air. He saw all these things – saw them and noted them, before the darkness swirled up to meet him and he fell down into it, a blessed relief.

EPILOGUE

HENRY DOYLE KEPT well back from Dr Cumby, the police surgeon. It wasn't that he didn't like Dr Cumby (insofar as anyone liked him), but the old man was cutting into John Whittaker's chest with an unseemly gusto, and Doyle would rather not get in his way. He nodded at Inspector Devlin, standing just behind him; the inspector had contracted a bad cold on a recent case and was wrapped up to the ears in an astonishing array of mufflers. He didn't speak, but watched the autopsy proceedings with keen interest, unfazed by either the mess or the smell. "Nothing like the sights to harden a man," Doyle remarked.

Devlin smiled. "Just here to observe, Mr Doyle, nothing more." He watched as Cumby sliced Whittaker open from pubis to sternum, extending the cut in a Y-shape towards each of the shoulders. The syphilitic deterioration was really quite remarkable, and Devlin marvelled that Whittaker had been able to keep going as long as he had. Part of his lower jaw was missing, the flesh eaten away from the bone, the tongue a suppurating sore. The muscles showed marked erosion, the skin puckered at the bends of the elbows and the hollow of the throat. The eyes were wide open and unseeing, just below the neat bullet wound in the forehead. John Whittaker was well and truly dead.

Devlin had a letter that he kept, secreted away in a locked box underneath his bed. It had come to him from Australia, shortly after Whittaker had left. Whittaker must have stayed up all night writing it, for the thing was twelve pages long, written on both sides of the paper. *You think you've got away from me, but I know better. Even now I'm watching you and I'm waiting for you. I'll have you yet, you wait and see if I don't.* He had detailed their long association in writing, and Devlin found himself marvelling at the tenacity of the other man's memory. He recalled pleasant things that Devlin had long since forgotten: games of cricket on school grounds, half-holidays and picnics, a ride in the headmaster's carriage one Christmas. He'd written it all down like a story, precise in every detail – but it was his version of events, a perversion of the facts, a collection of anecdotes with all the bad bits carefully suppressed. It reminded Devlin uncomfortably of the more lurid broadsheets, with their tales of leering henchmen and outraged virgins. It was a narrative entirely worthy of Whittaker. Hard to believe that this wasted, emaciated corpse had wreaked such havoc in his time. He watched in silence as Cumby weighed and catalogued the internal organs: liver, lungs, heart. Of this last, Devlin was most surprised, for Whittaker's heart was huge, enormous, swollen to fully three times its size, glistening on the surgeon's weigh scales like succulent fruit. He watched as Cumby sliced and weighed while Doyle jotted notes, and in the end, Whittaker's organs were stuffed back inside of him and the body cavities sewn shut with sturdy butcher's twine. "Should you like me to cut you a souvenir, Inspector?" Cumby held up one of Whittaker's hands. "A finger, perhaps a toe? We can preserve them most amiably nowadays."

"No." Devlin took an involuntary step backwards. "No, thank you, Doctor."

"Best wash him, then," Cumby said. "I believe the sister will be coming later to receive his body for burial." He carried himself away with the inherent dignity of the very old, bearing his blood-soaked hands in front of him like trophies of war. He vanished into the washroom, mumbling to himself.

"And here's the man who killed poor old Lizzie Hobbs," Doyle said. He dipped the sponge into the water, turned the dead man's wrist. "That's an odd tattoo. I've never seen the likes of that before."

"I have," said Devlin. He touched it lightly with his gloved fingertips – HELL FIRE – and then he turned, and went away.

* * *

"Freddie, you don't have to keep bringing me things – I'm hardly on my deathbed." Devlin glanced up at the tall young constable hovering by his bedside. "The doctor says it's just pneumonia, and I shall be fine as soon as ever." He coughed, a terrible racking noise, and Freddie Collins moved to prop him up.

"I'm not going away. You can bloody rattle on as long as you like and call me everything, but I'm staying here to see to you." Freddie positioned the tea tray over Devlin's knees and poured a cup of the steaming brew. "Anyway, I've got some news that will make you happy." He withdrew a folded newspaper and handed it to Devlin. "Front page, three columns."

YARD MAN CLEARED OF CHARGES:
SIR NEVILLE ALCOCK TO RETIRE AT MONTH'S END.

Devlin grunted. "About bloody time." He slurped his tea, oblivious to social conventions. "And what did they say about . . .?"

"John Whittaker's case has been . . . indefinitely suspended." Freddie was smiling. "Violet will be very grateful." He frowned. "I don't entirely understand."

Devlin permitted himself an inward smile. "What is it you don't understand, Freddie?"

"Well . . ." Freddie laid the teapot down on the bedside table. "Violet did Whittaker, right? And good for her, because it was high time somebody did. And his wife was killed while he was up in Surrey chasing us, so did he kill her? Or did she kill herself?"

"It's entirely possible that he did kill Sarah," Devlin replied. "He might have killed her before he ever went to Surrey. Knowing the kinds of connections he had, he could have asked one of his minions to do it."

Freddie nodded. "But Sarah is dead and Whittaker is dead, so . . ." He shrugged.

"It's unlikely that the Yard will want to expend further manpower on what it regards as a closed case. And now that Sir Neville is retiring, well . . ." Devlin added a shrug of his own. "Violet was terrified of an open scandal. Poor girl – having to serve justice on your own flesh and blood that way . . . it can't have been easy for her." He was secretly glad that she had taken Phoebe and departed almost immediately for the United States. "They will be very happy in Boston, she and Phoebe."

"Boston?" Freddie was surprised. "Have they gone to America?"

Devlin sighed. "Boston is normally located in America, yes." He smiled. "And what better place to have a 'Boston marriage'?"

Freddie was quiet for a moment as he sipped his tea. "Is that what we've got," he asked, "a Boston marriage?"

"Gentlemen don't make Boston marriages," Devlin said, in a tone that would have done justice to Reginald Harker. "But I'll be here, Freddie, if you'll have me."

Freddie flung himself on to the bed with rather more vigour than was strictly necessary.

246 • J. S. COOK

"Have you a theory on why Whittaker started killing in the first place?" Devlin asked.

"A theory?" Perhaps Freddie's mental faculties hadn't expanded so very much.

"John Whittaker knew he was dying," Devlin said. "He knew he had a few months at best. He had been cheated of everything: his inheritance, his reputation, his position in Society."

"Sure you aren't reaching, Sir?"

"Men like Whittaker kill because they believe they've been wronged by society. They want someone to take it out on, and so they take it out on everybody. Whittaker was probably infected by a male prostitute, so he killed renters."

"But why kill Elizabeth Hobbs? I mean, why set her on fire and push her out a window?"

"Because she came to me for help." Devlin sighed. "She said a man had been following her, interfering with her. Norris Pence was police surgeon ten years ago during the Elizabeth Hobbs case. If Norris Pence was Whittaker's inside man then, he probably told him about her. I told her I could protect her. So Whittaker made sure I couldn't. It was his way of getting back at me."

"For what?"

Devlin wasn't proud of himself, wasn't proud of the secrets he was bound to keep because of the law and because of his sworn duty to uphold it. "I lied to you before, a lie of omission. When we were at Fowler Street that day, you asked me how I knew Whittaker's habits so well, and I said we'd been at school together." He examined a hangnail on his thumb, worrying it until the small thread of skin snapped. "We were at school together, but we were hardly what you might call friends. But then I met him again, just after he'd come of age. He was . . . different. He'd travelled, you see, done things that I could only dream of. It was very alluring, for a while. He blamed me for his disease because I threw him over. I had just joined the Force. I was afraid I'd lose my job if I kept on with him, so I broke it off. Shortly after he came back from Australia, I received a letter from him. He'd been infected with syphilis. He said I'd driven him to renters. He blamed me for his illness."

Freddie was quiet. "That's horrible," he said finally. "Having to go through that." He examined Devlin's face intently. "I wish you'd told me. You could have trusted me, you know. I can keep a secret. I'm good at keeping secrets."

Devlin knew he ought to say something insightful and profound, knew he ought to ask forgiveness, but the habits of a lifetime stilled the impulse. There was still such an astonishingly long way to go. "I'm glad you're here," was all he said.

And "here" was, truth be told, much better than Devlin's old lodgings, or Freddie's rooms, because "here" was a very nice flat near the Yard, with large windows overlooking the street and a fine tobacconist's around the corner, and plenty of good brandy and their fire. It was understood, of course, that Inspector Devlin and Constable Collins merely shared rooms in the interests of economy, and because they were both bachelors. Wasn't it a shame that the Inspector had been all set to marry Phoebe Alcock, and then she ran away to

Boston with some red-haired woman who was probably an actress, or at any rate, not a very nice woman, certainly not the kind of woman who is ever received in polite society?

Such a shame, really.

SOME OTHER READING

from

BRANDON

Brandon is a leading publisher of new fiction and non-fiction for an international readership. For a catalogue of new and forthcoming books, please write to
Brandon/Mount Eagle, Unit 3 Olympia Trading Estate, Coburg Road, Wood Green, London N22 6TZ, England; or Brandon/Mount Eagle, Cooleen, Dingle, Co. Kerry, Ireland. For a full listing of all our books in print, please go to

www.brandonbooks.com

KEN BRUEN
WINNER OF THE SHAMUS AWARD FOR BEST NOVEL, FINALIST FOR THE EDGAR, BARRY AND MACAVITY AWARDS

"Bleak, amoral and disturbing, *The Guards* breaks new ground in the Irish thriller genre, replacing furious fantasy action with acute observation of human frailty." *Irish Independent*

"Both a tautly written contemporary *noir* with vividly drawn characters and a cracking story, *The Guards* is an acute and compassionate study of rage and loneliness . . . With Jack Taylor, Bruen has created a true original." *Sunday Tribune*

ISBN 0 86322 281 1; Paperback

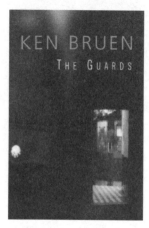 

"Jack Taylor is back in town, weighed down with wisecracks and cocaine . . . Somebody is murdering young male travellers and Taylor, with his reputation as an outsider, is the man they want to get to the root of things . . . Compulsive . . . rapid fire . . . entertaining." *Sunday Tribune*

"Upholds his reputation for edgy, intelligent, thriller noirs." *Ri-Ra*

ISBN 0 86322 294 3; Paperback

KEN BRUEN

"Outstanding. . . . Ireland's version of Scotland's Ian Rankin."
Publishers Weekly

"Irish writer Ken Bruen is the finest purveyor of intelligent Brit-noir."
The Big Issue

"Why the hell haven't I heard of Ken Bruen before? He's a terrific writer
and *The Guards* is one of the most mesmerizing works of crime fiction
I've ever read. . . This guy is the real thing." James W. Hall

ISBN 0 86322 302 8; Paperback

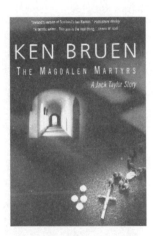
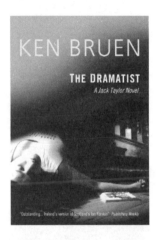

"Collectively, the Jack Taylor novels are Bruen's masterwork, and *The
Dramatist* is the darkest and most profound installment of the series to
date. A clean and sober Taylor – a man who has always been a danger to
his friends – proves infinitely more destructive to those around him. The
senseless death of a recurring character brings *The Dramatist* to a crushing
conclusion. The novel's chilling final image of Taylor could serve as a
dictionary illustration for noir. Readers who dare the journey will be days
shaking this most haunting book out of their heads." *This Week*

ISBN 0 86322 319 2; Paperback Original

SAM MILLAR
The Redemption Factory

Stunning crime fiction from the bestselling author of *On the Brinks*

A man is murdered, an anarchist suspected by his own group of being a police informer, but the killer has his doubts. Years later, in a deserted wood a corrupt businessman, Shank, silences a whistleblower, but the killing is witnessed and leads by way of brutal interrogation back to the first murder and its consequences. Lurking sometimes at the edge of the action, sometimes at the centre, is the deeply dysfunctional family of Shank and his two strange daughters, and their gruesome abattoir.

ISBN 0 86322 339 7; Paperback Original

KITTY FITZGERALD
Small Acts of Treachery

"Mystery and politics, a forbidden sexual attraction that turns into romance; Kitty Fitzgerald takes the reader on a gripping roller coaster through the recent past. In *Small Acts of Treachery* a woman of courage defies the power not only of the secret state but of sinister global elites. This is a story you can't stop reading, with an undertow which will give you cause to reflect." Sheila Rowbotham

"[*Small Acts of Treachery*] is a super book with a fascinating story and great characters. The book is all the more impressive because of the very sinister feeling I was left with that it is all too frighteningly possible."
Books Ireland

ISBN 086322 297 8; Paperback

KATE McCAFFERTY
Testimony of an Irish Slave Girl

"McCafferty's haunting novel chronicles an overlooked chapter in the annals of human slavery . . . A meticulously researched piece of historical fiction that will keep readers both horrified and mesmerized." *Booklist*

"Thousands of Irish men, women and children were sold into slavery to work in the sugar-cane fields of Barbados in the 17th century . . . McCafferty has researched her theme well and, through Cot, shows us the terrible indignities and suffering endured."
Irish Independent

ISBN 0 86322 314 1; Hardback
ISBN 0 86322 338 9; Paperback

 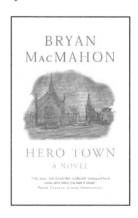

BRYAN MacMAHON
Hero Town

"*Hero Town* is the perfect retrospective: here the town is the hero, a character of epic and comic proportions. . . It may come to be recognized as MacMahon's masterpiece." Professor Bernard O'Donohue

"For the course of a calendar year, Peter Mulrooney, the musing pedagogue, saunters through the streets and the people, looking at things and leaving them so. They talk to him; he listens, and in his ears we hear the authentic voice of local Ireland, all its tics and phrases and catchcalls. Like Joyce, this wonderful, excellently structured book comes alive when you read it aloud." Frank Delaney, *Sunday Independent*

"*Hero Town* is a *Ulysses* for Listowel and it is more than a novel; it is a work of philosophy, the philosophy of a 'wild, old man', to quote Yeats." Gabriel Fitzmaurice

ISBN 0 86322 342 7; Paperback

MARY ROSE CALLAGHAN
The Visitors' Book

"Callaghan takes the romantic visions some Americans have of Ireland and dismantles them with great comic effect. . . It is near impossible not to find some enjoyment in this book, due to the fully-formed character of Peggy who, with her contrasting vulnerability and searing sarcasm, commands and exerts an irresistible charm." *Sunday Tribune*

ISBN 0 86322 280 3; Paperback

EVELYN CONLON
Skin of Dreams

"A courageous, intensely imagined and tightly focused book that asks powerful questions of authority. . . this is the kind of Irish novel that is all too rare." Joseph O'Connor

"Conlon tells the extraordinary and unusual story of Maud's search for the truth, a journey that takes her not only to Ireland's past but to contemporary America and death row." *Sunday Independent*

"This astoundingly original novel stunningly portrays the close bond between twins that can be so easily severed. From drunken nights in Dublin to Death Row, Conlon traces the tale of two generations, through life and death, justice and execution, obsession and love. A beautiful novel, which will move you by its courage in delving into controversy and its imaginatively spun revelations." *Irish World*

ISBN 0 86322 306 0; Paperback

JOHN B. KEANE
The Bodhrán Makers

The first and best novel from one of Ireland's best-loved writers, a moving and telling portrayal of a rural community in the '50s, a poverty-stricken people who never lost their dignity.

"Furious, raging, passionate and very, very funny." *Boston Globe*

"This powerful and poignant novel provides John B. Keane with a passport to the highest levels of Irish literature." *Irish Press*

"Sly, funny, heart-rending. . . Keane writes lyrically; recommended." *Library Journal*

ISBN 0 86322 300 1; Paperback

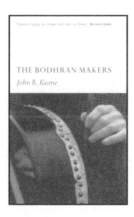 

DAVID FOSTER
The Land Where Stories End

"A master storyteller." *US Newsday*

"A post-modern fable set in the dark ages of Ireland. . . [A] beautifully written humorous myth that is entirely original. The simplicity of language is perfectly complementary to the wry, occasionally laugh-out-loud humour and the captivating tale." *Irish World*

"I was taken by surprise and carried easily along by the amazing story and by the punchy clarity of the writing. . . This book is imaginative and fantastic. . . It is truly amazing." *Books Ireland*

"Our most original and important living novelist." *Independent Monthly*

ISBN 0 86322 311 7; Hardback